# FATAL JUSTICE

## VIGILANTE JUSTICE THRILLER SERIES 2 WITH JACK LAMBURT

## JOHN ETZIL

*Another one for my Family*
*What else is there?*

Brooks having friends in low places were the two most requested songs. What can I say? Summit had its share of simpletons.

The locals drank beer and danced to their favorite songs until they were too drunk to move. Come closing time, they'd stagger and weave their way home, most of 'em staying on their side of the faded double yellow line that ran down the center of Route 10. It wasn't pretty, but that's all we had in our quiet little town, so we were happy to have it.

"Can I freshen that up for you?" the bartender asked. She looked at me with those sultry almond-shaped eyes, courtesy of her Japanese mother, that made me melt every time she made eye contact with me. I felt knee-wobbling weak around her, but I thought I did a good job of hiding it.

"Nah, I'm good for now. Think I'll play a little pool, though. Can I get some quarters?" I whipped out a five and handed it across the bar to Debbie. She sauntered over to the cash register and I admired the snug fit of her Levi's. I didn't bother raising my eyes or killing my grin when she turned around and came back with my night's worth of pool table money. She was used to me undressing her with my eyes, so she didn't bother to comment. Her sly smirk said it all.

She placed the quarters on the bar in front of me. "Good luck at the pool table," she said. "Those guys look like players to me." She gestured over to Max and Gus, the two old men that were smacking the balls around the beer-stained pool table as if they were playing bocce ball. "I wouldn't play them for money if I were you."

They were at least two times my forty-three years, but they moved pretty well and still had a bright sparkle in their eyes. Ice-cold beer worked wonders.

"Yeah, thanks. If I lose my pickup truck to them, I'll be counting on you to give me a lift home."

"Oh, I'm taking you home anyway, unless Frances over there gets to you first." She turned to the other end of the bar and waved, her arms swinging overhead like she was waving off an errant F-18 that was attempting to land on the deck of the USS *Stennis* on a stormy night.

I looked over and there she was. My number one fan. She must have been pushing ninety-five, but goddamn, she still drank whiskey by the shot glass. She sat ramrod straight on her barstool and sucked on a Marlboro Red. At least she'd switched from those filterless Lucky Strikes.

She caught me looking over at her and winked at me, an exaggerated gesture that looked like she was having a stroke. Oh, jeez. She waved and called over to me. I cringed, praying she wouldn't lose her balance and fall off of her stool.

"Sheriff Joe, come drink with me." She raised her glass and smiled. "I'm buying."

Sheriff Joe retired a few years ago. Nice enough guy, but aside from being about a foot shorter than me, sporting a walrus mustache that complemented his combover, and

Glock 17? Check, in my right hip holster under my untucked flannel shirt.

Spare magazines? Check, one in each cargo pocket of my Vertx tactical pants. A total of fifty-one nine-millimeter rounds. Wait a second. Fifty-one divided by three is seventeen. I love math. I could shoot each one of them exactly seventeen times. With my Glock 17. Hmm. Coincidence? I didn't believe in them.

Enough. Back to work on my mental checklist.

Osprey silencer? Check, left cargo pocket.

Cable tie handcuffs? Check, coiled up in my back pocket.

Swiss Army knife? Check, right cargo pocket.

Blackjack? Check, right next to my Swiss Army knife.

It might seem like I was sporting a lot of hardware, but when you're six foot six, you can get away with carrying an arsenal and folks won't notice. Even if they did, they wouldn't dare ask.

Attitude? Oh, um, not so good. I needed to work on that. The mental health experts say that the first step in solving a problem is admitting that you had one.

I had one.

I shook away the vision of shooting all three of them in the parking lot and stuffing their bodies in their trunk in a compromising sexual position before taking a photo, posting it on their Facebook pages, and driving their car into the woods and setting it on fire.

I grimaced and chastised myself for thinking such crazy

shit. Jeez, what the hell was freakin' wrong with me? I could start a forest fire, for God's sake.

I blamed my temporary lapse of judgment on the warm beer in my hand, looked down at it, and drained it before it could do any more damage.

The three of them finished their colored drinks, threw some cash on the table for Mary Sue's tip, and headed over to the bar to pay their bill.

Ostrich Boy tried to make eye contact with Mary Sue, but she ignored him. Good girl. Fatty stayed behind, dug into his pocket, pulled out another bill and dropped it on the table before falling in behind them. He must have felt guilty for his friend's behavior and wanted to make it up to Mary Sue.

Fatty and Skinny split the bill. Once they were done paying they just stood there, hands in pockets, while Ostrich Boy, hands moving a mile a minute, flirted with my Debbie. In the mirror behind the bar, I couldn't help but notice his bleached thousand-watt smile as he tried to woo her. I grinned at the thought of his expensive pearly whites being shattered by the heel of my boot as he lay unconscious in the parking lot.

My fantasy was interrupted when it dawned on me that during his entire conversation with Debbie, his two friends had stood with their backs to the bar, overlooking the crowd. They stood out like the Secret Service agents you see at political gatherings, except they didn't have those coily earpieces and weren't dressed as nice. I realized that they laughing hysterically like an overtired kid who drank too much caffeinated soda. He'd pull away, stop, wait for the two buffoons to come sliding through the snow and catch up to him, and pull away again once they got their meaty hands on the door handles.

The fatter of the two took a hard spill on his ass, his fat jiggling like a cartoon character. An "Ooh, shit" wheezed from his mouth when he landed, and he sat there breathing heavy in the snow for a second, dazed from the sudden stop. In his struggle to catch his breath, he sounded like he'd just sprinted a mile. In reality it couldn't have been more than fifty feet, but I had to cut him some slack because he probably hadn't run that far since he was in grammar school. If ever.

I had to work hard not to laugh out loud at the comic stupidity I was witnessing, and despite them bringing up highlight reels of the Three Stooges in my head, I knew these three dumb bastards were armed and dangerous. Especially Ostrich Boy.

According to HFS, a little known government spy agency, he was a stone cold killer who took special delight in torturing his victims until they pleaded with him to kill them. Then he'd torture them some more.

After another minute or so of proving his superiority, Ostrich Boy seemed to have grown bored of playing his high school game and he let the two cold and out of shape middle aged adolescents into the big Cadillac. I could hear him laughing when they opened their doors.

I walked over to my vehicle, started her up, and left my headlights off. The snow was light enough on my windshield that my wipers cleared it away in no time.

The big SUV made a quick left turn onto Route 10, and I followed them from a safe distance. They traveled less than a half mile before making a right onto Sawyer Hill Road. After a couple of hundred feet, they made a left turn into the parking lot of the Lakeview House, a small B&B that overlooked Summit Lake. Hopefully this was their last stop of the night. I drove past them and pulled over to the side of the gravel road.

During the day, Sawyer Hill Road didn't have much traffic on it. This time of night it was downright desolate. I got out and walked over to the Lakeview House, arriving just in time to see the three stooges stumble up the front steps.

Once they were inside, I watched them through a window on the front porch. They bypassed the small bar that greeted you as soon as you entered and headed up a flight of stairs to the second floor, which housed the guest rooms of the old house. They moved out of sight, and a couple of lights came on within seconds of each other. The three clowns had entered their rooms. Hopefully for the night.

I went back to my truck and sat for a while, watching in my side-view mirror to make sure that nobody left the Lakeview House. The last thing I wanted to see was any of them returning to the Red Barn.

Maybe the SUV didn't belong to Ostrich Boy, and was just a coincidence? But I didn't believe in them, so I crouched low and stayed in the shadows as I approached. I needed to get close enough to read the license plate without being detected. If it was a match, I needed to see how many people were inside the big SUV. After that I could formulate a plan.

The temperature had dropped and it felt like it was well below freezing. With each exhale I could see my thick breath illuminated in the moonlight. I only had a flannel shirt on, but my adrenaline kept me warm and my Glock always gave me a warm fuzzy, so I didn't feel the cold. Long gone was that pleasurable feeling that came with fantasies of Debbie and me cuddling in front of my fire place.

I unbuttoned my shirt and tucked the right side of it behind my back and into my belt to give me unrestricted access to my Glock. I loved those guns. They had no safety, so with a little practice you could outdraw anyone. We didn't exactly live in Wild West times, but it was nice to know that when the shit hit the fan, you'd be fast on the draw and could fire without having to worry about thumbing off a safety.

When I reached the intersection of Route 10 and Charlotte Valley Road, I crouched behind a shrub on the lawn of the two-story clapboard house that sat on the corner. From there I could see the SUV up the street, and the Red Barn across from it. The SUV was no longer idling, and that concerned me. A lot.

Ostrich Boy and his buddies could be hiding in the shadows of the parking lot, which was lined on one side with shrubs. Even worse, they could be inside the Red Barn.

I was running out of time, so I made my decision. I grabbed my Glock and stepped out from behind my cover.

# 6

My first task was to see if the license plate matched. I stayed close to the bush line and crouched down as I approached the rear of the vehicle. My eyes had adjusted well to the darkness, and with the help of the moon it was easy to make my way without tripping over the old broken up sidewalk. But I couldn't read the license plate until I was almost on top of it. Might be time for glasses.

I held out hope that it was a false alarm, that the plates would be from some lost soul from Arkansas. Then I could jog back to my truck and be on my way in no time, the whole episode being nothing more than a small delay that wouldn't make a difference in the night's pleasure that awaited me. Finally at about three feet away, I could make out the license plate. King Rex. Damn.

Tinted windows prevented me from seeing inside, so I had to make a decision. Did I risk walking around to the

front of the vehicle to see inside? If someone was inside, I'd
be an easy target. Did I create a distraction, try to lure them
out? I'd give away my advantage of surprise if I did that. I
could forget about the SUV for now, assume that all three of
them were here, and sneak around to look in a back
window of the Red Barn to see what was going on inside.
But if they had a lookout, I risked being spotted. I couldn't
rush the decision and make things worse, but I couldn't sit
around all night either. I knew that at least one evildoer was
here.

I made my decision and walked over to the tree line in
the back of the parking lot. I planned on following it to the
rear of the building and looking in some windows.

I'd gotten about half way there when the door to the
Red Barn opened, and Debbie and Mary Sue stepped out,
acting as if everything was normal. That made me feel
better. They stopped and chatted, and I mentally urged
them to get in their cars and drive away, but my telepathy
was shooting blanks and they stood there gabbing. Sheesh.

Finally, Mary Sue made a laughing comment about
freezing her buns off and the two of them got in their vehi-
cles and started them up. Their windshields were covered
with snow, so they got out, gloved them clean, and got back
in and waited for the defroster to do its job.

From behind I heard the big Cadillac engine start up. I
realized right away what had happened. Ostrich Boy was
going to follow one of them, probably Mary Sue, and I had
made a critical error by being so far from my vehicle. If she

took off now and he followed her, I'd never be able to get to my truck in time to follow them. I chided myself for my rookie mistake.

My adrenaline doubled down and my heart raced, pounding so loud in my ears that I swear everyone within five blocks could hear it. I holstered my Glock and tore ass down the street toward my truck in a full-blown sprint that would have made Usain Bolt stand and cheer.

I had a good three hundred feet to go before I reached St. Anna's parking lot when from behind I heard a car creep across the snow-covered gravel lot of the Red Barn. I turned around just in time to see headlights swing around and head in my direction.

I needed to hide, fast, otherwise I'd be seen. I saw a row of small evergreens and dove behind them, sliding on my stomach in the snow, just as Mary Sue's VW sped past me. She was going way too fast on the slick road. I'd have to have a chat with her about her driving habits.

It was close, but I wasn't spotted. A couple of seconds passed and I saw what I was afraid of. The Cadillac SUV pulled out of Charlotte Valley Road and followed Mary Sue's car on Route 10.

When the SUV passed me, its big four-hundred-horse-power engine roaring loud to accelerate the three-ton machine, I peered in the side window and saw a single occupant. Ostrich Boy.

## 7

DEBBIE STILL HADN'T LEFT the parking lot yet, but when she did she'd be heading my way. I didn't want to take a chance on her seeing me, but I had no choice. I had to get going in my truck before I lost Ostrich Boy.

The defroster gods were on my side and they took their time clearing the windshield of Debbie's BMW. I made it back to my truck and with wheels spinning and kicking up snow I tore ass out of the church parking lot and onto Route 10. I looked up in my rearview mirror and saw the familiar sight of Debbie's halogen headlights pulling out from the parking lot. That was close.

I accelerated and pulled away, impressed with my little Toyota's power as I passed through seventy-five, tightened my seat belt, and backed off when I touched ninety. The roads were wet from the fallen snow, but not yet frozen. At least not where I was, but it wouldn't surprise me to start running into frozen patches of road. The squiggly "Bridge Freezes Before Roadway" sign popped into my head and I tried to remember if I would be racing over any of the thousands of small bridges that crossed the many streams and creeks that meandered through upstate New York. I drew a blank. Damn warm beer.

I rounded a slight bend and spotted the taillights of the SUV and backed off the gas. I didn't want to get too close and get made. Some law enforcement officers might actually opt for that. One of the techniques for thwarting emotional crime, which this was a case of, was delay—the thinking being that the longer the interaction between attacker and victim was delayed, the more likely that the aggressor would get over his anger towards his victim and move on. I could pull up to the SUV with my lights off and force him off the road, sending him to the hospital for the night.

I didn't believe in that theory. Not even close. I'd listened in on enough illegally tapped phone calls to understand that you never gave these guys a second chance. If you had an advantage, like the one of surprise that I had now, you used it.

I resisted the urge to pull up alongside him and empty my Glock into the side of his face. While that would be satisfying, his dead body would bring unwanted attention, so I had to be patient and see what developed. I knew that

Mary Sue's house was still a few miles away, but I didn't know what Ostrich Boy's plan was. I did know that it wasn't good, and that he was going to die tonight. Other than that, I was at a loss.

In one stretch of road where Route 10 upsloped and curved slightly, I could see the SUV stalking Mary Sue's car in the same view. The short little greasy-haired bastard was doing an admirable job of keeping a safe distance from her so that he wouldn't be spotted, and I used the time to think through possible scenarios.

Would he force her off the road? I doubted it. Too risky. Someone could drive by, see them, and offer assistance. Or just drive by, keep going, and now you had a witness.

Would he follow her to her house and break in after she went inside? That was risky too; Ostrich Boy had no way of knowing if anyone else was home, and everyone in Summit, and most of upstate New York, had at least one hunting rifle handy. I had a .22, a .223, a .30-06, and a twelve-gauge shotgun. And lots of ammo. Glock was my pistol of choice, and I had three 17s, one in each bedroom, all locked away in quick access furniture safes. I had dozens of 9mm spare clips lying all over the house, like most homes had ashtrays in the seventies.

The more I thought about it, the more I became convinced that he'd follow Mary Sue to her house and kill her. And anyone else who happened to be there.

Armed or not, before the average American homeowner

her signal and pull into her driveway. I used my emergency brake to stop so that my brake lights wouldn't give me away, and killed the engine. I'd be hoofing it from here.

I took out my Glock, screwed on my Osprey silencer, and stepped out into the cold night.

## 8

I USED the tree line along the side of the road as cover, and within thirty seconds I arrived along the side of his SUV.

It was empty.

I'd expected as much. He hadn't driven out here to sit around in his car. I hadn't quite figured out what I was going to do if I found him in the SUV, but I knew that it would be bad for him. And bad for me if I got caught, but I'd been in this game a long time, and if there was one thing I was really good at, and I mean Super Bowl Champion good, it was getting away with murder.

Mary Sue's house was set back about a hundred and fifty feet from Clapper Hollow Road. The long, winding stone driveway ended at a two-car garage in a modern colonial. They had already decorated for Christmas, with a well-lit outdoor manger scene that included three full-size kings bearing gifts. Along with the soft glow of the outdoor lights, it looked like a Hallmark holiday card.

No sign of Ostrich Boy, but I'd figured as much. If I were in his shoes, I'd be at the back of the house by now, searching for a weak entry point.

With tingling nerves and my Glock leading the way, I snuck up the side of the driveway furthest from the house. There was a light smattering of snow on the driveway, and I could make out what appeared to be two sets of fresh tire tracks in the snow. Damn, that wasn't good. That meant that someone had either just arrived, or just left. God, I hoped they'd just left. But who would it be? Her parents were away and she didn't have any siblings. Boyfriend? Girlfriend? I'd find out soon enough.

I was in the zone, every cell in my body in tune with the sights and sounds of the night. It was too cold for the cricket serenade, so the only sound I heard was my own hiking boots compacting the snow with each step.

The closer I got to the house, the brighter it became, and I could easily see that there were two sets of tire tracks in the snow. I rounded the last curve in the driveway. Bad news.

Two cars were parked in front of the garage. One was Mary Sue's, and the other was a late-model Ford Mustang, its windows clear of snow and the hood still warm. Her boyfriend's car? A friend? Didn't matter. It was still another innocent person that had to be dealt with.

I went to the front of the house and looked through the

windows to see if Ostrich Boy was already inside. There was some risk in that, if he was hiding in the woods, maybe having second-guessed his adventure, or more likely still trying to plan out his attack with his pea-sized brain, he would see me and have the upper hand. But I didn't figure a guy like him for well-thought-out actions, so I went ahead.

I had to dodge the rectangular shafts of light that illuminated the snow-covered lawn. It seemed like each room in the house had a light on. I'd have to have a little chat with Mary Sue about wasting energy too. Maybe her parents weren't as perfect as I thought.

Feeling like a Peeping Tom, I knelt down before I reached the first window and raised my eyes up, just above the sill in the corner, to peek inside. Nothing. I ducked my head, crawled to the next window, and repeated my slow-motion jack-in-the-box routine. Nothing, except snow-soaked knees and frozen hands.

I went from window to window until I'd covered the whole length of the front of the house, not seeing any signs of life from within.

I continued around the corner of the house, knowing that if I came up empty, I'd work my way around the back. I'd find him there. If not, I'd find his entry point and follow him in. I didn't look forward to a confrontation inside the house, but I didn't want to be here to begin with either, and look how that worked out.

The side of the house was dark, something that I was

thankful for. I stood up and stretched out my stiff back. All this crawling around on hands and knees was for the birds.

I didn't see anyone through the two windows on each side of the massive brick fireplace, the clear focal point of the family room. There was a tall Christmas tree against the far wall, and it cast a holiday spirit glow throughout the room. "Silent Night" played in my head.

I worked my way around to the rear of the house and peered around the corner. I watched for a while but didn't hear or see anything in the backyard.

I saw a gigantic multilayer deck on the back of the house with a wide staircase that came off the corner at a forty-five-degree angle. The deck led up to an all-glass double slider, something I might have to come back to.

I walked around the outside of the deck and headed over to take a peek in a bay window that I figured would give me a view of the kitchen. I knelt down as I got closer, peeked through the corner, and there they were.

## 9

Mary Sue was sitting in a kitchen chair against the far wall, her hands tied behind her back with what looked like electrical cord. Her ankles were tied to the leg of the chair. Her face was bruised and there was some blood on her white server's shirt. She was stifling her sobs, her eyes shut, her body shaking.

A kid who looked to be college-aged sat next to her, and he was tied up the same way she was. He was big, not quite my six foot six inches, but pretty close. Muscular too, almost Greek god-ish in his physique, and probably weighed more than my two twenty. He had his head hung low and he was crying. A mixture of drool and blood dripped from his mouth.

Ostrich Boy paced back and forth before them, gesturing with his hands. I couldn't make out what he was saying, but I was sure that whatever it was, it wouldn't make the final cut of a Hallmark card selection.

I grabbed the handle of the sliding glass door, Glock pointed at him in case he heard me. I didn't want to double-tap him in the chest inside Mary Sue's house, but I would if I had to. I slid open the door so slow that it seemed to take thirty seconds to create enough of an opening for me to step through. Good thing I wasn't fat.

I stepped inside the carpeted family room. Up two steps and I'd be in the kitchen. I prayed that Mary Sue wouldn't give away my presence with her eyes.

She looked up and saw me, but there was no change in her facial expression. Good girl. If this college thing didn't work out for her, she had a bright future as a poker player.

Ostrich Boy had stopped pacing and stood in front of the kid. "This your fuckin' boyfriend?" He shook his head side to side, and even with his back to me I could see the disapproval in his body language. He reared back and smacked the kid in the face.

"No, please stop." The kid choked back sobs. "Please let me go, I won't tell anyone, I promise."

Ostrich Boy smacked him again. "You're a freakin' pussy." He was right. The kid was much bigger than Ostrich Boy but mentally he was a submissive pansy. I fought hard to stop the sigh of disgust from parting my lips. What a waste of a powerful physique.

Mary Sue's tone was soft and calm when she answered him between sniffles. "No, he's just a friend."

Thank God. If this clown was her boyfriend, I'd have to have a heart-to-heart with her about that too.

"Just a friend, eh? You fucking whore, this is what happens when you dis me." He reared back and slapped her across her face with his open hand. He laughed, unbuckled his dress slacks, and dropped them to his ankles. "Now the fun starts." He grabbed her by the hair, yanked her head back, and stepped in closer. "Open your mouth."

I tiptoed up behind him. The crying kid noticed me and let out a yelp. Jeez, he *was* such a loser. Ostrich Boy saw the kid looking past him and stopped what he was doing. He turned around so fast that he nearly stumbled. Good thing he was wearing those fancy boots to keep him from stepping out of his dress pants.

# 10

OSTRICH BOY'S eyes bugged out when he saw me, but it was too late for him to do anything. I kicked him in the nuts, a direct hit—not an easy task for such a small target, and I patted myself on the back for my expertise in accuracy. Bruce Lee would have been proud.

The violent smack of leather on the fragile genital skin disturbed even a hardass like me. Yuck. Sometimes I hate my job. I made a mental note to acid-wash my boots with a wire brush when I got home.

He grabbed at his crotch with an *oof,* and I slammed the Glock against the side of his head. He collapsed forward on the kitchen floor with a thump, out cold, his hair still perfect.

I kicked him in the right side, just below his rib cage, driving the tip of my boot into his liver, a penalty kick for forcing me to see his fat ass naked and making me touch his junk, even if it was just with the tip of my boot. Proxy and all.

Crying kid screamed again. I looked at him, shook my head with a sigh of disgust, and placed the tip of my Glock silencer six inches in front of his nose. "Shut. Up."

His red-rimmed eyes widened and the blood drained from his face. I thought he was going to hyperventilate and pass out from fear, but somehow he managed to stay conscious.

I cable-tied Ostrich Boy's hands behind his back, and pulled his dress slacks up. I rolled him over to his back and buckled his eight-hundred-dollar diamond-studded leather belt extra tight around his chubby gut.

I wiped the butt of my pistol all over his silk shirt to get the oily slick from his hair off. It left a nice little pattern on his five-hundred-dollar shirt. Even though it was petty of me, I couldn't help but chuckle at my abstract work of art. Picasso had nothing on me.

I patted him down for weapons and felt a mass in his front right pocket. I reached in and was rewarded with a compact Ruger 380 pistol. Nice. I popped out the clip, saw that it was fully loaded, re-clipped, and shoved it in my pocket.

I stuck my hand into his other pocket and found a smartphone. I wasn't worried about anyone being able to place his phone at this location because there was no cellular service here on this side of the mountain.

I grabbed his right thumb and placed it on the phone's

fingerprint reader to unlock it. I changed his pass code to 1234, tested it to make sure that it worked, then shut it off and put it in my pocket. This would come in handy later.

I took out my Swiss Army knife and cut Mary Sue's bindings. She wiped a tear from her cheek and smiled at me. She stood up, her legs wobbling like a newborn colt, and gave me a hug. I felt her whole body trembling. I held her until she stopped shaking, for what seemed like a full minute.

"Who's that?" I nodded over to crying kid.

"Harold." She leaned over to untie him. "We're just friends."

*Thank freakin' God.*

"Don't touch him," I said. She stopped and looked at me. "Why not?"

I gestured toward him with my Glock. He jumped and yelped. Again. "Can he keep a secret?" I raised a questioning eyebrow. "Go to his death with it?"

"Yeah. I can keep a secret. Yeah. Of course I can. Just untie me," he interrupted.

I pointed my gun at him, again, and he got a close-up peek inside the tip of the silencer. His eyes widened, and I saw his pupils grow in fear. I might appreciate the inner workings of such a wonderful noise-deadening piece of art, but I didn't think he did.

"Shut up. Understand?" He nodded his head up and down. "Good. When it's your turn to speak, I'll tell you." I nodded my head up and down, trying to convey to him the universal *yes* gesture that I expected of him. It worked, and he mimicked my motion. I nodded my appreciation. He had officially risen to equal the IQ of my dog London.

Mary Sue's forehead was wrinkled in confusion. "Secret? What do you mean?"

"We can't go to the cops with this guy." I nudged Lard Ass with my foot.

"What? Why not?"

"Guys like this, hardcore mobsters, they don't play by the rules. They don't follow laws. They'll never stop coming after us and we'll never be safe. We'll be dead before we can testify against him. Your family will never be safe."

"How do you know he's a mobster?"

"Believe me, I know." I bent down and searched for Ostrich Boy's wallet. The fabric of his dress slacks was so soft that you could make a baby's blanket out of it. I had to admit, the sick bastard did have good taste in clothes.

I found his wallet and took it out of his pocket. It was made form baby seal leather. Figures. I opened it, found his license, and memorized his name and address for future reference. Then I handed it to her.

"Get your laptop, open TOR, and search for Sam Rexanio."

"TOR? What's that?" she asked.

"It's an untraceable web browser for people who want privacy. It doesn't leave an Internet browsing history on your computer and it routes your Internet connection through multiple servers so that it's untraceable."

She ran off to get her laptop.

Now was a good time to have a little chat with Harold. I pulled up a chair, sat down in front of him, and laid the Glock on my lap, pointed to the side so he didn't think I was trying to intimidate him.

"So, can you really keep a secret?" I asked, watching closely for the physical "tells" of lying that the untrained body doesn't know enough to hide. Things like rapid eye blinking, a change in posture, voice inflection, fidgeting, and a couple of others that didn't apply since they involved hand gestures that couldn't be accomplished when your hands were tied up like Harold's were.

"I can, I won't tell anyone, I swear. Now please untie me."

Harold was a terrible liar. He exhibited every single physical tell I knew of, including some I hadn't thought were possible with hands tied up. I felt like I was watching a CIA video tutorial on spotting deception. The only thing missing besides a narrator was freeze-frame red circle graphics around all his giveaways.

"Harold, Harold, Harold. Sorry to say, buddy, but I don't think you understand the gravity of our situation." I laid my hand on the Glock. "Now, in a few minutes, Mary Sue's gonna come in here with her laptop and show us a little bit of history about our friend here." I gestured toward Sammy with the gun. "I think once you see for yourself who this douchebag is, you'll be a little more convincing in your ability to keep secrets until your death."

He stared at me but didn't speak. His lips were trembling and he'd developed a nervous tic in his shoulder.

I pointed the gun at him. "So, I'm going to ask you one simple question. Do you think you can keep an open mind and read what Mary Sue's going to show you?" I nodded my head up and down again, and he mimicked me. Yep, he was definitely in London's league. I set the Glock back on my lap and nodded my appreciation to him.

"Good answer."

Mary came hustling into the room, her laptop cradled in her arms. "I've found him!" She placed the laptop on the kitchen table and turned it towards us. "Holy crap, you won't believe how evil this guy is."

## 11

I was curious to see what Google brought up from the newspapers about Sammy and how accurate it was. If they had even ten percent of the story right, these kids were in for a rude awakening. Even someone as daft as Harold would have to agree with me.

"First we go to Google Images, to make sure that we have the right guy," Mary Sue said. She clicked on the "Images" tab, and after a long delay caused by the TOR browser routing us through multiple servers to protect our location and identity, photo after photo came up of our Ostrich Boy.

At nightclubs dressed to the nines, walking in the street with a guy on each side and two behind him. At charity events, hobnobbing with politicians, getting into and out of limos, etc. Hundreds of them, proving that the clown on the floor was indeed Big Sam Rexanio of New York.

"Now we know it's him, so let's go to the news. Here's where it gets good." She clicked on the "News" tab, and a host of articles appeared on the screen. Most were recent, and a few included mug shots. He didn't photograph well.

Every major newspaper from the *New York Times* to the *Washington Post* had numerous articles implicating Big Sam for extortion, murder, gambling, racketeering, loan-sharking, dog kidnapping, etc. Lots of indictments, few convictions, and even fewer jail stays. He seemed to have a guardian angel watching over him. I smiled. *Not anymore.*

Mary Sue looked at me. "So what now?"

I looked at Harold. "Do you understand who we're dealing with here?"

"Maybe he'll be thankful for us not killing him, and leave us alone," he said.

Mary Sue rolled her eyes. "Jeez, are you for real? Didn't you see what this guy was going to do to me?"

"Yeah, but I'm sure he wasn't going to kill us. If we'd just played along, this could be over. But not now." He gestured to me with his head. "Thanks to your friend here."

I fought back the urge to bitch-slap him and instead let him continue his imbecilic rant. "He attacked a big-time mobster. Well, I'm not taking the fall for him."

My restraint ended, and I reached for my Glock. Mary Sue placed her hand on my arm.

"Don't." She looked at me and shook her head slightly.

I didn't say anything.

"Okay, Harold." Mary Sue turned back towards her

friend, stooped down, and spoke to him like he was a ten-year-old. "Let's just say that *we* played along. Do you think guys like this ever leave a witness to a crime? Someone who could testify in court against them?" She paused for added effect, then added, "They don't. Which is why he has all those indictments against him, but hardly any convictions. Are you getting this?"

He waited a few seconds before answering. "So what now? We just going to murder him in cold blood?"

I'd had enough. I took the Glock and stuck it in Harold's face. He whimpered like a scared puppy. I silently apologized to London for lumping this moron in the same category.

Mary Sue shrugged and surrendered the reins to me. She was good. "Sorry, Harold, I tried." She walked away and stood at my side with her arms crossed over her chest.

"Wait, you just can't let him shoot me." His voice quivered and cracked like an overly excited preteen.

"I'm not going to shoot you...yet." Now it was my turn to pause for added effect. "So here's how this works. I'm leaving with Sam. Mary Sue will untie you after I leave. This way, you can't be implicated in removing the body. And this whole night never happened. Capiche?"

"Ka-what?"

"Capiche. It's Italian for 'got it?'." God, this kid lived a sheltered life.

"I don't know, man, this whole thing sucks."

"Yeah, it does. And it will play out in one of three ways.

We go to the cops, and Sammy kills us all. Or: I leave with Sammy, and you tell someone what happened, and I kill you before you can testify against me. Not that I'd need to, because my word as Sheriff is much more believable than yours. But I would anyway. I mean, why take chances, right?"

I let him think for a minute, then continued; "Or: I leave with Sammy, you man up and live with our little secret for the rest of your life, and nobody else dies. And I can guaranfuckin-tee you, that the first option ain't gonna happen. Capiche?" I stuck the Glock in his face and nodded my head up and down, delighted with my new expertise in subliminal coercion.

Sammy groaned and rolled over, but didn't open his eyes.

Harold looked down at him. "What are you going to do with him?"

"Does it matter? All that matters is that he'll never bother us again, and that you're not involved. The only thing that you did is keep a secret. Now grow some fucking balls, look me in the eye, and swear on your mother's grave that you'll take our secret to *your* grave."

Harold thought for a second, and a sigh of resignation seeped from his lips. He looked up at me. "Fine. You win. I'll never tell anyone. Ever."

"Excellent. Oh. Almost forgot. There's one more thing."

"What's that?"

"You're never to see Mary Sue again."

"What? What the hell?" He sounded like he was going to cry. Big surprise.

"You're a nice boy, but you have a lot of growing up to do before you're man enough to hang with her." I stood up and stuck the Glock in my belt.

I remembered that Sam's SUV was far away and I needed to retrieve it. I asked Mary Sue, "Any open bays in the garage?"

"Yeah, one. Do you need to pull your truck in?"

"Not my truck, his SUV. Can you move the car that's blocking the open bay?"

"On it." She grabbed her keys and trotted over to the door that led to the garage.

She came back two minutes later. "All set, door's open too."

"Good. Do you have any plastic drop cloths?"

"I think so, in the garage. I'll check." She came back a few minutes later with a clear plastic drop cloth, the kind a homeowner would use for a painting project.

"Excellent. Sit tight, I'll be right back." I grabbed Sammy's keys and hiked out to his SUV, hopped in, slid his seat back, and started her up. I drove into the garage and shut the door. So far, so good.

When I stepped into the kitchen, Sammy was wide awake, sitting up, and talking to Harold.

## 12

"YOU WERE RIGHT, kid, I wasn't going to hurt you. I was just having a little fun." He smiled at Harold and tried to stand up. Mary Sue stood behind him, frozen, her skin pale and her eyes the size of saucers. My eye caught the glint of the ten-inch butcher knife that she cradled against her chest with both hands.

I took out my Glock and made eye contact with her from the doorway. When she saw me, I swiped my head to the right, indicating that she should back up from him. She understood my gesture right away and took two steps back. Smart kid.

I felt relief, not wanting her to go through life with the heavy burden of having killed a man. Not just killing, but stabbing, which was just so damn intimate. Unless you had the reach of Andre The Giant, you'd wind up being close enough to breath in their last breath. I hated that.

Plus, the average body holds one and a half gallons of blood. I looked down at the kitchen floor and noticed the small gaps between the vinyl tiles that would act like magnets to his spilled blood. It would take us hours to sop all that mess up. I'm in great shape and all, but four hours on my hands and knees and my lower back would be sore for a week. Screw that.

Sam continued his used car salesman pitch, complete with ear-to-ear grin. "All's you got to do is let me go and you'll never see me again. I promise. Scout's honor. So what do you say?"

I gingerly stepped into the kitchen and crept up behind him. I was in plain view of Harold, but he never looked at me. Good boy. He was learning. I got within arm's reach and smashed my Glock into the back of Sammy's slicked-back head. He collapsed like an old abandoned building being demolished with dynamite.

I grabbed the plastic drop cloth, shook it open, and spread it out on the floor. I rolled Sammy up in it.

"Oh God," Harold moaned, as if the visual of Sammy's face disappearing under the opaque plastic drove home the seriousness of the situation.

I took my time wrapping him up. The less DNA and greasy hair follicles I left behind, the better. I dragged his fat ass out to the garage and heaved him into the back of his SUV. I closed the hatch, happy to be getting this douchebag out of the house, and Mary Sue's life, forever.

I went back inside and instructed Mary Sue, "Wipe the

floor down with a strong cleaning solution. Think of anything he may have touched and wipe that down too. Anything. Doorknobs, countertops, tables, chairs, toilets. Then burn the paper towels you used. I'm leaving." I waved the Glock over at Harold. "Call me if he gives you any trouble." I pointed the pistol at his chest. "I'll come back and finish him off." I winked at her and left.

## 13

THE BACK of Sammy's head hurt like he'd been whacked with a Louisville Slugger. When he'd first opened his eyes and realized he was still alive, he'd felt pure jubilation. The euphoria faded fast when he tried to move and realized that his hands were tied behind his back and he'd been rolled up in a plastic sheet. And he was lying in the back of a moving vehicle.

He recognized the new leather smell mixed with his favorite air freshener, forest pine, and realized that he was lying in the back of his own vehicle. His heart raced and his breathing picked up. Always a mild claustrophobe, he imagined the plastic tightening around his torso like a noose, constricting his breathing. His chest tightened and he wanted to scream out. His pulse quickened, and a cold, clammy sweat dripped from his body. Nausea hit him like a Mike Tyson body shot, and he felt faint. *Calm down, just breathe.* He closed his eyes and focused on slowing his breath and figuring a way out of this. He'd dug enough holes and buried enough rats in his life to understand what was happening. If he didn't get his shit together, he was going to wind up in a hole. Tonight.

But how? Why? Who knocked him out and tied him up? He remembered the big kid at the wench's house, but he couldn't be the law. Otherwise he'd be on his way to a holding cell, not wrapped in plastic and heading over to a hole in the ground off some backwoods trail. In his own SUV. How disrespectful.

Had he messed with the wrong guy? Unlikely. This sleepy little rat-fuck town had no made men in it. He'd checked with all his contacts to see if the guy he was gonna whack, a real estate developer with an art collection side business in the neighboring town of Cobleskill, had any connections. He didn't, and this town was clean as a whistle.

He couldn't say the same for the real estate developer. Eight months ago the sleazy little bastard sold him some artwork that turned out to be of questionable origin. So questionable that the FBI had come to have a little chat with Sam. Not only had the cheating bastard art dealer tried to pull one over on him, but he'd led the FBI to him.

Sammy was shrewd enough in his shady dealings to avoid convictions on most of the criminal charges that were brought against him, but that was a double-edged sword. It wouldn't take much for the bosses to think that he'd stayed out of jail because he was a mole. A visit from the FBI was the last thing he needed, and dropping in on the art dealer unannounced was payback for his little FBI meet-and-greet. And while he was here, he'd help himself to some artwork. For his troubles and all.

He took a deep breath and sucked in plastic. He struggled to move his face around so that he could breathe, and was shocked to feel the plastic start to unravel around him. What? His captors hadn't used duct tape to secure the plastic? Ha. What a bunch of fuckin' amateurs!

He felt the vehicle decelerate, and the smooth pavement ended with a jolt. His whole body became airborne for a second before slamming down with thud. The bouncing of the vehicle picked up, and they slowed down to a near crawl. They must have gone off road, which meant they were getting close to the hole.

He mentally raced through some survival plans before settling on the one he thought offered him the best chance of success. He had always been good at spur-of-the-moment improvising, a trait he hoped would prove its value again in extending his life.

## 14

"Are you okay?" Mary Sue asked Harold. She cut through the electrical cord that bound his wrists and ankles to the chair.

"Yeah, I'm fine, just in shock." He was shaking his head as if to wipe the slate of his memory clean. "Wow, that was close. Are you sure we're doing the right thing?"

"Positive. Besides, we gave the sheriff our word."

"I know, but he's a freakin' psycho."

"He knows what he's doing."

"It's fine until we get caught. Then we'll get jail time for covering up a murder."

She frowned. "You're looking at it all wrong. We didn't cover up anything. We just didn't report an assault that occurred in my home. End of story." She sliced through the last of his bonds. "There, all free. Now leave and never speak of this again."

"But what about us?" Harold sniffled and looked like he was about to well up. "Can I still see you?" He reached out and placed a hand on her shoulder.

She slapped his arm away. "No, Harold, it's over." Her voice rose an octave.

"Why?"

"You don't get it, do you?" She clenched her fists in anger, digging her nails into her palms. It was all she could do not to smack him in the face or kick him in the groin. She'd never in her life felt so little respect towards a living being as she felt now towards him. "That man was going to rape me and kill us both. You didn't even put up a fight. You did nothing, Harold. You were going to let him! Get out and don't ever contact me again."

She held the front door open and Harold shuffled out, his body sagging in despair. She slammed the door behind him so hard that all the family portraits rattled against the wall. She sat down on the couch and buried her head in her hands and cried.

I PULLED the big SUV out of Mary Sue's driveway and up to my truck. I hopped out and reached into my glove compartment. I found the lead-shielded bag that was originally made for protecting camera film from X-ray machines at airports. That didn't fly anymore. Nowadays you couldn't even get a Chapstick through security without a sideways glance from the X-ray operator.

Anyway, the reason I had this bag was to keep the locations of my burner phones away from prying eyes. Even though the cell phones were off, I knew that they could still be tracked, so I always kept a fully charged phone in the lead-shielded bag. One never knew when they'd need a burner phone.

I opened the bag and tossed Sam's phone inside, then sealed it up. There was no cell signal here, but as I got closer to Summit, I'd be picked up by a cell tower, so I figured better safe than sorry. As far as Verizon or AT&T were concerned, Sam had driven along on Route 10 into a dead spot and never returned. They didn't know how right they would be.

I grabbed my cleanup kit, which was nothing more than a Ziploc bag that held paper towels and hand sanitizer, and stuffed it in my back pocket. I locked my truck, jumped into the SUV, and threw it in drive.

It took me twenty minutes to reach my property in Eminence, and another thirty minutes to make my way through the tractor trail that connected my driveway to the back corner of my land, where it butted up against the million-plus acres of state-owned forest.

There used to be a small one-room cabin at the end of the trail, built sometime in the 1800s, but that was long gone. All that was left was a partially collapsed stone foundation, overgrown with weeds and small shrubs, with a couple of taller trees in the center of it.

And a hand-dug well.

Hand-dug wells in this part of the country ran anywhere from thirty to seventy feet deep, depending on the underground water level. They were usually about forty inches around and were lined with rock to keep the walls from caving in. This particular well hadn't been used in many decades and was covered with a two-inch-thick piece of flat stone. It would make a perfect burial place for Ostrich Boy. Once I filled it with dirt, he'd never be found.

I stopped the big SUV when I thought we were getting

close to the well. I hadn't been up here in a while, and that was during daylight hours. Everything up here in the country looked different at night. I got out and savored the dark silence. It was so quiet and peaceful, the only sound the clicking of the big engine as she cooled off.

I took out my iPhone flashlight and searched for the well. After a few minutes I found it, hidden by tall grass and a few short shrubs. I got back in the SUV and backed it up to the well, opened up the back, and pulled his fat ass out, letting him hit the ground with a nice satisfying thud. I grinned.

I bent down to slide the heavy rock from the opening. The thing must have weighed over a hundred pounds, and over the years it had sunk into the ground a half inch. It took some work digging my fingers underneath it, and it was covered by moss, so it was slippery and hard to grip. After a few tries and a half dozen curse words, I managed to slide it all the way to the side, opening up a three-foot-plus opening to his tomb.

I grabbed him by his feet, slid his fat ass over the snow to the well, and dropped him into it. Probably my imagination, but I could swear I saw him ball up before he disappeared into the darkness. It had been a long, exhausting day, and despite my stoic appearance, this exercise in body disposal was slightly stressful. Plus I had Debbie and Barry White waiting at home for me, and knowing that always increased my ADD tenfold.

A second later, I heard him splash down. My anger at

him got the best of me and I picked up a few bigger rocks from nearby and tossed them down the well, imagining them smashing against his greasy head. That didn't satisfy my thirst for revenge, so I took out my Glock, screwed on the Osprey, and fired a few shots down into the well as a parting gift. Between shots, I heard the empty shell casings bouncing off the rock lining of the well before splashing down. *Good riddance, you bastard.* I slid the heavy stone back in place and sealed his tomb. It felt good to be free of him.

I climbed back into the late Ostrich Boy's SUV and headed back to the Lakeview House. It took me almost an hour, and when I arrived, I parked the SUV in the lot, same spot as I had seen it in earlier. I took a few minutes and wiped the interior down with the sanitizer-soaked paper towels to remove any evidence of my existence, and left the key fob in the visor. I tossed the towels in the fifty-gallon burn can everyone in upstate New York had in their back-yard, tossed in a little extra hand sanitizer, and threw in a match.

I watched the beautiful blue and orange flames as they converted the last bit of evidence linking me to the SUV to black smoke and bits of ash that disappeared into the night sky. Environmentalists would go ape shit if they saw what I'd done.

I walked over to the trailer park down the road from the Lakeview House, and after sneaking up on a half dozen trailer homes, I found what I was looking for. A bicycle. Okay, it was bright pink and had fluffy little pink things hanging from the handlebar ends, but I wasn't in a position to be picky, so I hopped on it and pedaled away towards Mary Sue's house to get my pickup.

There was hardly any traffic on Route 10 at three a.m., but every time I saw the occasional car headlights I had to veer off and hide on the side of the road behind some bushes until they passed. No way I could let anyone see me. Not on that bike, anyway. I'd have to move to escape the ridicule.

Those little breaks in pedaling were a godsend because they gave me a chance to stretch out my long legs. The bike was so small that my knees rubbed against the handlebar with each stroke of the pedals, and I cramped up pretty quickly. At least I wore off those fluffy pink things with the friction. Hiding on the side of the road had the added benefit of allowing me to catch my breath. Those hills on Route 10 were murder.

The first half of the ride wasn't too bad, but when my body started to heat up from the workout, I started to sweat. It was near freezing, and by the time I reached the turnoff from Route 10 onto Mary's Sue's road, my clothes were soaked through with sweat. A breeze hit me, and I switched from overheating to freezing in about four seconds.

With each pedal stroke my frozen clothes chafed at the back of my knees, and I could feel the skin irritation forming through my impending frostbite. I didn't know which was worse, the friction burns on the front of my knees from rubbing against the handlebars, or the frozen rash on the backs of them. This killing stuff certainly wasn't for the faint of heart.

It took me almost two hours to bike from the trailer park to Mary Sue's house, and by the time I tossed the bike into the bed of my Toyota, my teeth were chattering and my whole body was shaking from the cold.

I started my truck, turned the heat up as high as it would go, and headed back to the trailer park.

It only took me ten minutes, but by the time I returned my girly ride to its rightful owner, minus its little fluffy pink things, the sun was peeking over the mountains.

Twenty minutes later I pulled into my long driveway and up to my log cabin. I saw that Debbie's car wasn't there, and my heart sank.

## 16

SAMMY DECIDED he would play dead until the car stopped and then see what happened next. He remembered only one man from that wench waitress's house, and he hadn't heard any conversation in the SUV. Maybe he was lucky and there was only one prick he needed to take out.

His first order of business was to get his cable tie cuffs off without making any noise that would alert the driver. He'd learned a long time ago to be prepared to escape from all types of situations, especially handcuffs. Traditional, cable tie, and duct tape varieties being the most common.

For most situations, the little two-shot Derringer pistol inside his right boot would be enough to save his ass. He pressed his ankles together and felt the familiar bulge of the tiny weapon. His killer had missed it. His spirits picked up and he went to work on his handcuffs.

A few months ago he'd received the diamond-studded

belt that he had on as a birthday gift from his wife, Sally. One of the first things he'd done was take a small eyeglass screwdriver and sharpen the tiny flat tip to make it razor sharp. He cut an inch of the tip off and slid it into a hole he had drilled into the inside portion of his belt. The hole was located in the middle of his belt so that it would be against his lower back.

If he was ever going to need it, his hands would likely be restrained behind his back instead of in front of him, but just to be on the safe side, he'd sharpened a second eyeglass screwdriver, cut that tip off, and hid it in the front of his belt.

The two wire-thin one-inch pieces of metal were so small and so well hidden that his belt passed though airport security with no problem.

But he had a problem now. Retrieving it.

His belt was on so tight that he could hardly breathe, and unless he created some space between his belt and lower back, he'd never be able to slide his hands in and get his lock-picking tool out.

He turned to his side, timing his action to coincide with the bumps they hit as they went from well-maintained roads to ones that had plenty of potholes. No good. With his fat gut pushing against his belt, it was impossible for him to get his meaty hands in.

He tried lying on his back and raising his hips to free his hands. With the help of gravity pressing his fat into his spine, the belt was loose enough for him to slip his hands under it.

A few minutes later he'd located the screwdriver tip. He'd spent the rest of the trip finger-wrestling the tip from its sheath, and within seconds of removal, he shoved the flat tip portion down into the cable tie's locking mechanism. The process was surgical and took some time, but he finally felt the cable tie loosen. Not enough to free his hands, but it was a good start.

The SUV slowed to a crawl, and stopped. He heard a door unlatch and recognized the door open chimes. Of all the insults, the bastard had stolen his car too. The door slammed closed. Shoot. This might be it. He worked at his cuffs with added incentive. He needed to free his hands before he was removed from his vehicle; otherwise he'd have no chance to retrieve the Derringer.

The door opened and shut again, and the SUV started up, maneuvered around, and came to a stop.

The door opened but didn't close. He could feel the cold air invade the toasty cabin. His SUV hatch beeped its opening. He struggled with the lock pick, his fingers trembling. *Come on, get these cuffs off.* Somebody grabbed him by the feet and started to pull him out of the vehicle.

Oh. Shit. This was gonna hurt. He held his breath and gritted his teeth as he felt his body slide out and scrape on the rear edge of his vehicle as he was pulled cleared of it. Knees, hips, waist, elbows, chest, almost clear. *THUNK.*

The back of his head slammed against the SUV's tow hitch so hard that he saw stars. Before the pain had time to register, his body hit the ground with a solid thud, the back of his neck taking most of the force. It took all of his willpower not to exhale with a scream.

He must have blacked out for a second, and when he came to, somebody had a grip on his ankles and was pulling him across the ground. He could hear the snow crunch underneath his weight as his plastic-covered body slid across it. He looked around but couldn't see anything through the opaque plastic except an out-of-focus shadow in the moonlight. One person.

The movement stopped and his feet were tossed to the ground. His heart rate picked up and he started sweating inside the plastic. This was his last chance. He put all of his faith in a single captor turning his back on him. To go get a shovel, to dig a hole, take a leak, whatever. At some point soon, he would have his chance. His body weight was pinning his hands to the ground, making it difficult for him to work the lock pick. He was so close.

He heard the sound of rock sliding against rock. Like the opening of an old tomb in an Indiana Jones movie. *What the?*

He slowed his breathing, pushed all thoughts from his mind, and focused on the cable tie lock. He found the slot, worked the tip of the screwdriver in, and felt the cable tie loosen. He slid one hand out, then the other. Yes. Free! Now he just needed to reach into his boot and...

His feet were hoisted up, he was pulled across the snow, and before he could react, the ground dropped away from underneath him. No! He instinctively balled up inside the loosening plastic, covered his head with his hands, and held his breath.

He tumbled the whole way down, his elbows and knees bouncing and scraping against the rock wall that lined his descent. As soon as he hit the water, he realized what had happened. This wasn't just a hole—he had been thrown into a well!

He hit knees first and continued tumbling as his momentum sank him towards the bottom. He fought his way free from the plastic. In the pitch-black darkness, and with all the turning he had done to get out of the plastic, he wasn't sure which way was up. He reached out and felt the stone wall. He heard a loud splash coming from one direction. That had to be the surface. But what were the splashes? Was it another body? The thought of sharing a hole with one of his goombahs freaked him out. He heard another splash. Shit. Not good.

He felt the bulk of a bowling-ball-sized rock brush against him as it made its way to the bottom of the well. He realized his killer was throwing rocks at him. What a piece of shit!

He reached out and grabbed at the wall and pulled himself lower in the water to protect himself. He heard what he thought were muffled gunshots echoing through the well, and he felt the vibration of the bullets as they burrowed into the water. His lungs were burning for air, but he didn't dare surface. In between gunshots, he heard the faraway sound of tinkling metal. It was the shell casings

ricocheting off the rock wall on their way down before plop-
ping into the water.

He stayed under as long as his lungs could stand,
surfaced just long enough to grab a fast breath, and went
back down underwater as quick as possible.

On his way back down, his heart sunk as it dawned on
him that there was no moonlight coming in at the top of the
well. It was pitch black.

He was entombed.

He followed the stone wall back to the surface and took
another deep breath. The well was pitch black and eerily
quiet, the only sound besides his chattering teeth that of the
occasional drip of water that echoed inside the rock-lined
chamber.

Hot flashes and nausea threatened to render him help-
less. This was like a bad dream that he couldn't wake up
from, and he had to fight to keep his claustrophobia from ·
taking over. The water was cold but still warmer than the
freezing outside air above ground. He lowered himself until
his lips were just above the water and felt around in the
dark for the diameter of the well to get a feel for its width.
He estimated that the well was less than four feet wide.

He probed the rocks that lined the well to see if he could
wedge his fingers in and get a good grip to climb out, but the
spaces between the rocks were too small, so he canned that
idea. Instead, he placed his back against one side of the well
and braced himself against the other side with his feet. If
this worked, he could inch his way up. He had to move

slowly in the pitch-black darkness, and it would take a long time for him to reach the top, but it wasn't like he had any choice. He got to work.

He reached down with his hands to about waist level, planted his palms on the rocks, and straightened his arms to push his torso up about a foot. He moved one of his feet up about six inches, set it firmly against the wall, and brought the other one up to meet it.

His ostrich boots were slippery on the wet rock, requiring even more leg strain to hold their grip, and his back was already sore from being forced into the uneven and sometimes pointy rock wall. But it was a start.

After struggling for what seemed like an eternity, he finally felt his butt clear the water and his boots drain. Fuck, this was gonna take a long time, but at least his little two-shot Derringer pistol in his right boot was out of the water now.

His Boy Scout training kicked in, and he reached down and felt around for the plastic sheet he had been wrapped in. It was floating near the surface of the water. He grabbed it and looped it through his belt. He'd need it later to help him survive the cold.

Mental focus was never one of his strong points, and he had three thoughts that kept interfering with his concentration of the task at hand.

How far did he have to climb? In the dark, he had no idea how far he'd progressed.

How much did that freakin' stone that sealed him in

weigh? Sure, he was strong, built like a bull, but in the awkward position he'd be in when he reached the top of the well, he might not even be able to move thirty pounds.

And, if he got out, how would he survive the frozen night while soaked to the bone?

# 17

At least London was happy to see me. When I pulled up, I spotted his gray-and-black face looking through the living room window. He was backlit by a nightlight that Debbie had been kind enough to leave on for me. Or that she had forgotten to turn off before she stormed out.

His tail was shaking so hard his head shook. Not the normal vision you had when someone mentioned "German Shepherd," but the superaggressive European guard dog of old had been bred down over the last few generations and turned into a great family dog. They're still fearless and the best guard dogs money can buy. Smart, too.

I pulled into my garage and entered the house through the mudroom. London hit the wall switch and the hallway lit up. I'd taught him how to do that in about ten minutes.

I let him out the back door and he ran around for a while, took care of some business, and tried to make friends with a couple of rabbits that were eating breakfast. They decided they'd rather hide under the shed until the scary black beast with the giant paws went away instead of risking life and limb for some wide-bladed grass or three-leaf clovers, so, he was left friendless.

He lay down under my hammock, a favorite resting place of his. Those rabbits really tired him out. After a few minutes he caught on that I wouldn't be coming out to relax at my prized napping venue. He trotted into the house, his big brown eyes happy to see me.

I spooled up the Keurig—hadn't gotten around to teaching him that yet—and made a cup of dark-roasted Colombian. London followed and lay down at my feet. He was still out of breath from frolicking with the rabbits and I made a mental note to take him back to the vet. On our last visit, the Doc commented that his heart murmur was getting louder, and that we needed to keep an eye on it. Not sure what we could do, London being almost ninety in human years and all...

I went to my workstation and started my TOR browser. After the normal delay to ensure privacy, I logged in to the HFS portal. HFS, commonly known as Home Front Security, is a top-secret federal agency. So secret that the folks who work there had to sign an agreement never to tell anyone who they really worked for, or what they actually did. I knew, because I'd had to sign one.

The agreement stayed in force for life, and every employee was given a custom-made cover story of their job duties. Mine was as a computer specialist for the State Department. If we told anybody about our real job, we forfeited our pension, turned over our firstborn, and were rewarded with an all-expenses-paid extended vacation to Leavenworth's version of Guantánamo Bay. I wasn't sure if waterboarding was part of the Club Fed package, but I wouldn't have been surprised if it was. Not to gain any intel, just to do it for the fun of it. And practice.

HFS had been started after 9/11 and was tasked with gathering information. On everyone. We didn't discriminate. We spied on every single person. If you had a pulse, we knew how many times a minute it beat. We were the gods of information gathering.

We unofficially labeled HFS "Holy Fuckin' Shit," because that was the reaction every single congressman and women had after we showed them examples of our intelligence-gathering capabilities during budget season. You would have said the same thing.

Everything—phones, TVs, Wi-Fi routers, microwave ovens, watches, refrigerators, thermostats, washing machines, water meters, satellite dishes, cable boxes, even your wife's Tampax—is our electronic probe into your privacy.

But the grand pooh-bah, big daddy of the mac of all eavesdropping devices, is the smartphone. Thank you, Steve Jobs. That's right, thanks to a little secretive strong-arming by our Twitter-happy president, *all* manufacturers implant a chip in every single device. Every one. That chip allows HSF to log in to your smartphone whenever we want, to listen, record video, and even check your email. Think you're safe when your phone is off?

Wrong!

Want to know what Joey in Connecticut was doing at 8:21:30 last night? The little devil had used his mother's credentials to log in to her laptop while she was out on a date, and was on RedTube watching two MILFs going to town on each other on a sixty-foot yacht while the owner drank champagne from their shoes.

At least Joey was smart enough to delete his browsing history before he shut down. Amazing how smart middle schoolers are these days. Too bad he didn't know about TOR, though...

While little Joey was learning about life on the high seas, Father George in Michigan was penning an email to one of his parishioners explaining why the rectory needed a new furnace. After a glass or two of red wine, he had this strange habit of typing in the nude. I had to admit, I hadn't expected such bravado from an Irish priest. Given their, ahem, shortcomings and all.

At least the good Father's alleged trafficking of old men for sex slaves turned out to be false. He also deserved credit for good posture while typing, back and head straight as an arrow. Part of that comes from his discipline of typing for twenty minutes and standing for five.

I scheduled my breaks to coincide with when he stood up, rationalizing that if I saw him naked one more time I'd be scarred for life and have to go on disability. At least now I knew why he'd become a priest.

The president was taking a little personal time with the first family and watching *A Christmas Story*. He slapped his knee and laughed like a little kid when Ralphie said "fudge." It was good to see him relaxing and enjoying life for a change.

Senator XXXXX was hosting a full-blown orgy in an oversized hot tub in D.C. while her husband was visiting his elderly mother in California. Her twenty-years-her-junior lover was a big hit, and easily won the night's MVP award. Amazing what a little Coke and Viagra could do for one's recuperative powers. I toyed with the idea of adding myself to the guest list for her next shin ding, but chickened out.

Dr. Klein was... oh, you get the idea.

HFS knows whatever they want to know, about anybody, anywhere. Nobody is safe. If you think you're safe, email me and within a few minutes, I'll get back to you with what you had for dinner last night, how regular your bowel movements are, your flaccid penis length, and how much you dial back your scale to convince your wife you're following her low-carb diet recommendations. Shame on you.

Act right now and as a special bonus I'll even let you know what percentage of her orgasms are fake.

So how is that massive amount of data organized and archived? That's where experts like myself come in. My master's degree is in IT security, and when I first graduated Notre Dame, I went to work for the CIA.

After a few months of working there I got bored with analyzing foreign activity, so I transferred to NSA. My excellent work ethic, plus my father's millions in political donations, made me pretty popular and labeled me as an up-and-comer in my secretive little D.C. tribe.

When the idea to form HFS was approved by the president, complete with plausible deniability, my name was thrown in the hat. Together with a handful of others who could keep a secret and had no immediate family that might call the police in case we went missing, we ran the most secretive organization in the history of the planet earth. Holy shit, that was fun.

But all good things end, and I have since moved on to the greener pastures of sheriffdom. I couldn't be happier. Watching Father George type emails in the nude was surprisingly stressful. I couldn't even tell any of my friends about it. Horrible.

And even though I'd bailed on that life, I kept my hand in the money jar via consulting work. Besides the easy cash, my second job of IT consulting for the government, while not as fun as my third job, had a ton of perks.

I could take on as many or as few assignments as I wanted. I could work from home. Evenings, weekends, sick days, middle of the night when I couldn't sleep and ran out of Jack Daniels. Whenever I wanted.

But the single most important thing that kept me in the IT game, besides lightning-quick body fat percentages and STD checks on potential lovers, was that I had access to all the data that HFS paid me to protect. I knew everything. About everybody.

With that treasure trove of data just a few keystrokes away, I had my pick of the litter, the belle of the ball, to choose from when I got the itch to live out my childhood Batman fantasies. Thanks to Kalib and Flight 2262, I got that itch a lot. That was unfortunate for people like Fat Sam, because, and I'll be the first to admit this, I didn't handle my God complex very well...

## 18

I LOGGED in to the HFS portal and within minutes I had Sam's file open on the screen. I studied it for a while, and when I grew tired of reading what a pitiful waste of life he was, I decided to find the two stooges from last night.

They'd have to try and find Sam. I mean, it wasn't like they could just drive home and tell everyone that Sam had disappeared into thin air. I chuckled out loud. London raised his head and looked at me like I had a tomato-sized tumor on the tip of my nose.

That would be perfect though. I could see them in my mind, hemming and hawin, doing a little two step in front of the big boss. "Er, ahh, uhm, sorry boss, we lost Big Sam. He just got up in the middle of the night and disappeared. Honest."

Right. I'd give them two days before they were whacked in retaliation for killing Sam.

But since that wasn't likely to happen, I figured the chances were good that the two hammerheads would reappear today at the last place Sam had been. The Red Barn. Where else could they start looking for him? I decided that I'd better learn a little bit about these jokers. Know-your-enemy type of thing.

Compared to Sam, their files were tiny. Fat Boy was married, lived in Staten Island, and was a low-level associate, as opposed to a "made man," which was mobster lingo for a fully initiated member. The only reason he was in Summit this weekend was because two of Sam's closest pals had recently enrolled in the witness protection program and were spending their days in warm and sunny Arizona, posing as a retired government employee and a florist. Seriously, can't make this stuff up. A florist?

Skinny Guy was a mob associate, single, and lived in Long Island. He'd spent much of his life below the radar, so there wasn't much background info on him other than a few arrests for some minor stuff.

Now I had to decide how to handle them. I'd opened up a can of worms with Sam's well tossing, not that I'd had any choice in the matter. But how much would this fiasco spin out of control? If I did nothing, the two stooges were sure to do something bad for somebody. Not for me. Probably for Mary Sue. They were desperate, and desperate men were very dangerous.

If I took them out, something that I salivated over like

Fatal Justice 87

the Big Bad Wolf did when he saw Little Red Riding Hood skipping through the woods all by herself, then we'd have even more visitors from their hood.

Unless... *Hmm, yes, that's it! I got it!*

# 19

LESS THAN HALFWAY up the well, Sammy's legs started to shake. Not from the cold, which was becoming a factor despite his body heat rising from the workload, but from the strain of keeping his lower back pressed against the rock wall hard enough to support his weight. His thigh muscles burned worse than he'd ever felt in his life.

He stopped and tried to lock his knees in place to support his weight, giving his legs a rest, but the well wasn't wide enough for him to fully extend his legs. He tried another tactic, and placed his hands on top of his knees and pushed against them so that he could relax his legs. Ahh, that felt good.

It lasted about fifteen seconds before his triceps gave out, and he was back to using his leg muscles to support himself. Holy shit, that was freakin' brutal. He extended his arms straight down, locked his elbows, and dug his palms into the rock wall next to his fat ass. He was able to take some of his weight off his legs that way.

He thought of Sally, and what a good and loyal wife she'd been throughout his rise in the business. Being the wife of a high-ranking mobster was difficult, and she had ulcers to show for it. Despite how it was portrayed in Hollywood, mobster life was anything but easy.

Sure, there were parties, and the work itself was easy. There was always lots of cash floating around. Mobsters were the ultimate "bad boys," and there was no shortage of gold diggers ready to hop in the sack with him and suck some cash from him.

All mob wives knew that their husbands' Friday nights with the boys were really Friday nights with their mistresses, but those whores didn't really *mean* anything to him. Plus he could do things with his girlfriends that he'd never do to the mother of his child.

And then there was his daughter, Barbara. Daddy's little girl, except that she was going off to college next year. Fuck, how time flew. She'd need him around to keep all those asshole boys from trying to jump her bones.

God, he loved them, and couldn't bear to leave them like this. Getting whacked was one thing. They all lived with that elephant in the room on a daily basis, but disappearing altogether? His family would never know what had happened to him. How would Sally handle his disappearance? She'd probably hold out hope for a while, but sooner or later she'd have to move on. How soon before she found another man to take care of her? He pictured a faceless man on top of her, pumping away to satisfy her, and his blood boiled.

Revenge was a powerful motivator, and his adrenaline surged at the vision of tracking down the big bastard from the wench's house and shooting him in the back of the head. He was a pro, and he'd do it the right way. He'd show that fool how to whack someone.

He thought of his Derringer pistol in his boot. It might have weighed in at less than eight ounces, but he'd used it over a dozen times, and each time it had worked flawlessly for close-up head shots. The little .22-caliber bullet was powerful enough to get through a thick skull, but not too powerful where it came out the other side and created a hell of a mess of splattered bone fragments, blood, and brain. He'd learned that the hard way when he'd used a .38-caliber on his first hit and spent the remainder of the night cleaning up the mess. That sucked.

Not so with a .22, though. The little bullet just bounced around the inside of the guy's head and created Swiss cheese out of his brain. He smiled.

His anger and lust for revenge fired him up, and the cold, fatigue, and red-hot burning of his leg muscles faded to the background.

He started inching his way back up the well. *I will kill that bastard. I will kill that bastard.*

## 20

THE ANXIETY SAMMY felt about being able to make his way to the top disappeared when his head brushed against the stone that covered the well. Yes!

His exuberance was short-lived, replaced by another fear. What if the stone was too heavy for him to move? How messed up would that be?

He rested for a second and started thinking about Sally, Barbara, and revenge, and his adrenaline started pumping again. He placed both hands on the stone and pushed. It didn't move; instead he felt his back slide down the rock wall. Shit. He cringed and stopped pushing. He placed his palms against the rock by his butt to support his weight and leaned forward to take some of the pressure off his back. He had to do this. He couldn't come this far and not make it.

He needed to find a better way to brace his back, so he felt around the perimeter of the well for a rock that stood out a little more than the others. If he found one and could work his way over to it, he could plant his ass on it and use it as a ledge, which would give him more leverage. Maybe even enough to move that damn stone.

About halfway around the well, he felt a small ledge of a rock. It stuck out about two inches from the others around it and was a little higher than he wanted, but he was in no position to be picky. He maneuvered over to the rock and slid his butt over top of it. He was closer to the overhead stone than he wanted to be, and his head was forced to the side, but he had to make do.

He reached up, held his breath, and pushed.

The stone didn't move. Damn. But his butt didn't slide down either, so that was a win.

This was it—he either moved this freakin' stone or fell back down into the well and rotted here. Fear and anger were powerful motivators. His heart raced and he yelled like a Russian weightlifter on steroids, and pushed with all of his might.

The stone rose.

He was able to slide it about an inch to the side before it settled back down, but the tiny victory pumped him up even more. He felt like Superman. He took a deep breath and pushed again, this time sliding the rock more than three inches to the side. Yes, holy shit, he was going to make it! He could feel victory within his grasp. "Woo." He grunted and pushed against the stone again. He slid it over another few inches, and the soft light of the rising sun streamed through the barren trees and lit up the well. He exhaled, and relief swept through him. He'd made it.

His right foot slipped off its supporting rock, and his torso tilted in that direction. He stuck his right hand out to stabilize himself. His left leg buckled under the pressure of the added weight and he fell back into the well, cursing all the way down as he entangled himself in the plastic sheet hanging from his belt.

## 21

EVEN BEFORE HE splashed down in the cold water, complete with brand-new cuts and bruises from bouncing off the rock wall on the way down, he knew that he'd get out of the well.

Once free of the plastic sheet, he wiped the water from his eyes and looked up at the shaft of light that pierced the blackness of the well and smiled. The moving of the stone had been the final piece to his escape puzzle.

Now he had the sun to help him as well. The yellow rays, with their promise of warmth, added an element of normalcy to the situation and elevated his mood to the point of euphoria. His pain and fatigue disappeared. Nothing could stop him now.

He took a few deep breaths through grinning lips and went back to work. *I will kill that bastard.*

With the promised warmth of the sunlight calling for

him, Sam made it to the top of the well in no time. He was amazed at how much difference a little light made in foot and grip placement, finding rocks with bigger grips than others, and overall mood improvement. He felt like he'd just done a line of coke and was about to attend his first female-only orgy where all eight women would be fighting to get their hands on him, like they were waiting on line for the stores to open Black Friday.

When he reached the top, he placed one hand on the rim of the well and the other hand against the stone. He pulled on one arm and pushed with the other, and the stone slid open enough for him to slither out of his tomb.

Holy shit, he'd made it. He stood on solid ground for the first time in hours, and took a deep breath. The cold, fresh air and the pumping adrenaline invigorated him. He felt like a god. He wanted to scream out, to rejoice at the top of his lungs, but thought better of it just in case the bastard who'd dumped him in the well was within earshot.

He looked around and studied his environment. Other than a few Boy Scout treks as a kid, he'd spent his entire life in urban areas, where vehicle traffic, sirens, and the normal hustle and bustle of city life created a never-ending symphony of sounds that all blended together. He'd gotten so used to hearing them that he didn't notice them anymore. Here it was the opposite. The quiet tranquility of dawn in the early-winter forest was so foreign to him that it put him on edge and made the hair on the back of his neck stand up.

He saw trees, many of them evergreens, and with the light dusting of snow reflecting the early-morning sun, the scene reminded him of a Christmas card. There were some smaller shrubs, most of them bare of leaves, and a small narrow path. He noticed tire tracks in the snow that led down the path. The tracks continued as far as he could see, and he realized that was the way he had been brought here. And his way out.

He thought about walking the path, but his whole body shivering reminded him that his clothes were frozen to his skin, and if he didn't get dry and warm real quick, he'd die from hypothermia. What a waste that would be, after all he'd been through.

He shook out the plastic sheet, freeing most of the water from it, and folded it up. After a lengthy inner conversation that lasted way too long for the seriousness at hand, he decided to swallow his manhood. He draped the plastic sheet over his shoulders to form a knee-length shawl, and looked over his shoulder to make sure that no one was around to see his feminine clothing faux pas.

He pushed the stone back over the well and trotted over to an evergreen tree and broke off a branch. He walked back to the well and smoothed the snow out to cover his tracks in case that bastard who had thrown him down the well came back. The dry snow moved easily under the breeze created from the waving evergreen branch, and he smiled at his ingenious handiwork.

He backed away from the well in the opposite direction

of the path, all the while fanning his tracks clean like an expert outdoorsman.

He'd gone about fifty or sixty feet when the ground sloped away at such a steep angle that he thought he'd slip and fall. He kept going, but at a much more careful pace, until the clearing around the well area disappeared from his line of sight. He continued for another fifteen minutes, memorizing landmarks so that he'd be able to navigate his way back to the well area later and pick up the path that would lead him out of here.

When he was satisfied that he was far enough away from the well, he gathered some dead tree limbs. He cleared the snow away by dragging his foot along it and scavenged for some dry leaves. Most of the underbrush was moist from the snow, but after scraping away the top layer, he found some that were dry and would be easy to start a fire with.

He went over to the biggest evergreen he could find, something that would help hide the smoke as it rose from the fire, and shook off the snow from the branches he could reach. He cleared the snow away down to the leafy ground, creating a small fire pit. He laid the dry leaves down in it. He threw a handful of twigs on top, and placed some dead branches on top of the twigs.

He searched for his lighter and had a brief moment of panic when he couldn't find it. In the last of his pockets, he felt the cold metal and smiled in relief. Now he just needed for it to work after being soaking wet for hours.

He took out the lighter, its gold casing reflecting the

sunlight, opened it, and thumbed the flint. It lit on the first try. He set the dried leaves on fire, and in a few minutes the damp twigs dried out from the heat and started burning. After a few more minutes, one of the bigger branches started to go up in flames and he sat down, his plastic shawl under his butt, ensuring that he didn't get any wetter. With his back leaning against the evergreen, he warmed himself by the fire.

Thank God for the Boy Scouts.

## 22

---

SAM'S EXHAUSTION from being up all night and the adren-aline dump that followed his climb out of the well was bone-deep. He fell asleep in front of the fire within five minutes of sitting down. When he woke up an hour later, the front of him was almost dry, but his back was still wet and cold.

The fire had died down, so he needed to get some more fuel to feed it. He closed his eyes and listened to the silence, making sure there were no out-of-place sounds. He stood up and gathered an armful of dead branches and placed them on the embers. After a few minutes, they ignited, and before he knew it the fire was hot enough to make him sweat.

He tried to swallow, but his throat felt like sandpaper. What irony, spending all night in a well and waking up thirsty. He looked around and spotted a small oval-shaped indent of sunken snow by the fire. It was about the size of a softball and it contained a few inches of water. He leaned over and examined it from different angles. It looked as pure as anything he'd ever seen. He grinned, placed his lips on the surface of the water, and sucked his mini-pond dry. Ahh, that hit the spot.

He stood up, removed his plastic shawl and spread it on the ground. He stood on it, his back turned to the fire, enjoying the warmth that spread across him. He was well rested now and felt rejuvenated.

He removed his boots and socks. He draped the socks over his boots and placed them close to the fire so that they'd dry fast. He took off his shirt and pants and laid them closer to the fire. He took the little Derringer from its ankle holster and examined it. It was damp, but he knew it would work. He placed it on the ground and took off his ankle holster and placed it down near the fire.

He lay down on the plastic and rolled the part furthest from the fire over his body for warmth. He flashed back to waking up in the back of the vehicle wrapped in plastic and had a whole-body shiver before shaking the claustrophobic thoughts from his head.

He sighed. For the first time since he was a kid, he enjoyed the simple things in life that he'd normally take for granted. Heat. Water. And shelter in the form of a little plastic sheet.

But his contentment didn't extinguish his anger. *I will kill that bastard*, was his last thought before falling asleep.

## 23

A FEW HOURS LATER, Debbie arrived at work and opened the Red Barn for lunch. She hadn't heard from Jack and was still pissed about last night, and she caught herself slamming the fridge door in anger. Him and his damn work. She knew what it was like to be married to her job, and while it had been exciting in her twenties, she'd grown tired of the one-dimensional emptiness of her life.

Next month it would be two years since her boss had tapped on the side of her cubicle, asking to see her. Her heart had pounded in excitement as she'd followed him down the hallway to his corner office. She'd just returned from an overseas assignment where things had gone well. A good, clean op. She'd expected an "attaboy" or maybe even an award for her mission success.

Instead, she was told that her parents were dead.

They were killed by a drunk driver on Route 88 just

outside of Albany. After the initial shock subsided, she requested and received a three-month leave of absence to come home to Cobleskill and clean up their affairs. She'd never left.

And she'd never once looked back. If anything, she regretted spending so much of her early years working so hard.

Foreign travel and eighty-hour workweeks were the norm, and her stress levels were though the roof. Since she'd been here, her quality of life had been a thousand times better. Too bad it had taken her parents' death for her to realize it.

That was what annoyed her so much about last night, when Mr. Married-to-his-work had ditched her. She shook her head and sighed. What the hell could be so important in Summit, New York, that he had to work? Freakin' A.

She refilled the bar supplies, pulled the chain of the neon Budweiser sign a little too hard, and sat down behind the bar. She took out her phone to text Jack, frowned, and put it back in her pocket. Screw this.

The door squeaked open and her first customers of the day, two burly corrections officers from the Summit Shock Camp, strode in and sat down at the bar. They were regulars at the Red Barn and stopped by a few days per week for supper after working the midnight-to-eight shift plus a little OT.

"Hey, Debs, how goes it?" Rodney asked.

Debbie smiled at him and placed a napkin and a cold

draft in front of him. "Awesome," she lied. "How about you guys?"

He shrugged. "Ah, I'm okay. You know how it is, another night in the shock camp jungle."

She put a second draft on the bar for David, who looked up from his paper and nodded his thanks. He took a mouthful and "aahh'd" his appreciation. She smiled at him and turned to start their tab.

Rodney admired her Levi's, and a grin spread across his bearded face. "I'm much better now, though."

She turned around and he raised his beer to her with a wink.

"I bet." She turned around again and pretended to do some work while she watched him study her ass in the mirror. He tilted his head to one side, like a dog trying to figure something out. She flicked her long, straight black hair behind her back in an exaggerated motion for his benefit and tied it up in a knot, turning sideways while her hands were still behind her head. Her breasts strained at her T-shirt, and she saw Rodney elbow David out of the corner of her eye. He hit him so hard that he almost spilled his beer.

David looked up at Rodney, saw his intense straight-ahead stare, and turned in time to catch Debbie's profile. His mouth opened.

She turned and looked at them, an "I caught you red-handed" smirk on her face, and asked, "You guys having the usual?"

Red crept up Rodney's neck and under his beard before blanketing his cheeks. "Um, yep." They both looked down and drank from their mugs.

She wrote down their order and delivered it to the kitchen with an exaggerated bounce in her step. She came back and they made some small talk. The typical male bravado blossomed after only half a beer. Like Rodney's "When you gone leave that sheriff and date a real man?"

"Soon as I find one." Her standard reply, which came with an over-the-top disappointed sigh, as if she'd never find one. *Although after getting stood up last night by Mr. Married-to-his-work, I might start looking for real.*

They bantered back and forth until the cook rang the bell, letting Debbie know that their food was ready. She served them and left them alone to eat in peace.

Two men she recognized from last night walked in. Holy cow, they looked like crap—unshaven, with bed head, wrinkled, slept-in clothes, worry lines painted across their oily foreheads. Must have been one tough night. She wondered where the third guy was. Probably still sleeping it off.

They nodded to Rodney and Dave and walked down to the other end of the bar and sat down.

Debbie walked over with two napkins and smiled at them. "Morning, gentlemen. What can I get for you?"

"I'll have a Coke and a burger," the fat one said, rubbing his face with his hand. "Extra fries."

The skinny one raised a finger and said, "Same here."

"Sure thing." She wrote down their order, dropped it off in the kitchen, and got them their Cokes.

The skinny one yawned and rubbed his hands through his hair. He lit a cigarette and exhaled the first drag with a whispered groan. "Oh, man, what a freaking nightmare." He sounded like he'd just been diagnosed with lung cancer and been given four hours to live.

The kitchen bell twanged and Debbie grabbed their burgers and set them down in front of them. "Anything else I can get you guys?"

"No. We're good," the fat one mumbled through a mouthful of fries. "Oh. I do have one question, though. We forgot to tip our waitress last night. Is she working today?"

"Yeah, Mary Sue comes in at four."

"Thanks." He smiled, opened his mouth wide enough that Debbie could see his tonsils, and shoved the burger in with both hands. *Maybe Jack's not so bad after all...*

Debbie turned and walked away. Hmmm... that was odd. After they'd closed last night, Mary Sue had told her that "those three guys were asses, but at least they tipped well."

After the lunch crowd emptied out, she grabbed her phone, typed a quick message, and hit send.

## 24

I was going through Sammy's smartphone and reading his texts while holding it inside the lead-shielded bag. It was cumbersome work, but I had to make sure his phone wasn't picked up by a cell tower.

A new text alert went off on my phone. It was from Debbie. My heart rate sped up and I smiled. I hadn't heard from her since last night, and I was getting a little worried about us. I swiped and read the text. Shit. Not what I'd expected. I'd assumed that it was an "I miss you and can't wait to jump your hot body" text.

Instead, I got a simple "Call me. Now."

I did, and in a workmanlike fashion, she filled me in on her lunchtime visit from the two stooges. Then she hung up.

I continued going through Sam's phone and reading his texts. Most of them were boring everyday stuff, with a low-

IQ twist to them. Around three thirty, I turned off his phone and closed up the lead-shielded bag. I jumped in my pickup and headed towards Summit.

My plan was simple. Thanks to HFS and my conversation with Debbie, I knew that hammerheads one and two would be at the Red Barn after four this afternoon to interrogate Mary Sue. I needed to observe them and make sure she was okay, but based on what I'd read on Sammy's phone, it didn't look good. The dumbass had told his stooges what he was up to last night, even mentioning her by name. Of course he'd spelled her name wrong. I shook my head in disbelief. I mean, come on, how could you possibly spell Mary Sue wrong? Poor bastard must have been dyslexic...

I arrived at the Red Barn a few minutes before four and parked on Charlotte Valley Road. From my stakeout position, I could see the parking lot, and there was no sign of Ostrich Boy's SUV. The sun would be setting in about half an hour and the dusk lighting lent a peaceful ambience to the whole scene. Unfortunately for the inner photographer in me, the gravel parking lot had no lights, so I had to go inside the Red Barn and wait.

I walked in and spotted Debbie behind the bar right away. She didn't notice me, so I took a seat at a table on the other side of the room next to a small window that overlooked the parking lot. Although the lot had no lighting, I could see cars as they came and went, and the single outdoor light next to the entrance was bright enough for me to be able to see faces right before a person entered.

I looked over at Debbie, a mild knot in my stomach. She was chatting with one of the corrections officers from the shock camp, who was parked on a stool in the corner. My corner. I watched them for a few minutes.

She preened nonstop, tossing her hair, redoing her ponytail. Her breasts drew his eyes like magnets to high-grade steel whenever she looked away to see if anyone needed a refill. He especially liked when she reached down into the cooler, the one in front of my stool, to grab a cold beer for a customer. Maybe it was just me, but it seemed she was doing it in slow motion. He inched forward in his seat, stretching his neck to gawk at her cleavage. His eyes widened and his jaw dropped so far I thought that he was gonna whack it on the bar top and knock himself out.

My neck heated up, and I had to remind myself that I had bigger things to worry about besides a girlfriend who happened to have a job that demanded flirting. If only she wasn't so freaking good at it. Or so hot. I silently vowed that my next girlfriend would be repulsive even to Shrek. Then I wouldn't have to worry about men lining up to hit on her like they did with Debbie.

"Well, look who it is." Mary Sue came over and inter-rupted my self-inflicted torture. Her gait was tense and her face stoic. "Long time no see." She had an icy mug with my name all over it in bold. She put down a Budweiser coaster and placed my beer on it. I grabbed it.

"Yeah, how are you?"

"Fine. But I think we might have a problem."

"I know, Debbie told me what happened at lunch. Just stay chill, I'll handle everything." I tipped my mug to her and winked.

"I know you will. And that's your last beer for tonight, so you'd better milk it. You can't afford to be slow on the draw."

"I'm two hundred and twenty pounds, it's gonna take a lot more than one beer to have any effect on my reflexes. But if it makes you feel any better, this will be my last one."

"Good." Her smile disappeared and she turned serious. She cleaned in a little closer. "How'd it go last night?"

"Done."

She breathed a sigh of relief. "Thank God for you, man, that's all I have to say, thank God for you." She raised a fist and we bumped. "Man, do I owe you." She smiled for the first time today.

"No sweat. Just stay chill tonight and make my job easy. You do that, and I'll owe you. We'll be even."

"Ha, I don't think so, but yeah. I promise." She grabbed her server tray and went to leave, but stopped midstride. She turned around and looked at me, held my gaze, then stepped in close and whispered, "Be careful."

I nodded and smiled, trying to make it appear to the other patrons that she'd said something lighthearted and witty.

She went over to the next table and introduced herself to an older couple. The place was starting to fill up, and I noticed Frances over in her usual place, a freshly lit Marlboro Red in one hand, a whiskey in the other. God bless her. We should all be so lucky.

The door creaked open and the two stooges walked in and went right towards Mary Sue. They sat down at a table and when she walked by them the fat one tugged on her sleeve.

My table was two over from them. It was too early for the band, so the jukebox was on, but it was on the other side of the dance floor, so it didn't interfere with my ability to hear the conversation. I caught bits and pieces of it. Enough to know that for two nights in a row, I'd be getting rid of a dead body. Correction. Bodies.

## 25

I SAT with my side to them, pretending to veg out while I nursed my beer. I kicked back, crossed one leg over the other, and tried to sink into the background and appear about as nonaggressive as a six-foot-six guy could. Slouched shoulders, head down. All-around pitiful example of how a man should carry himself. Kind of like George McFly from *Back to the Future.*

Mary Sue walked away from them, cool as a cucumber. I listened.

"Think she's lying?"

"I don't care if she is or isn't. We take her after she gets off from work and cut the fuckin' truth out of her."

"Do we really need to do that?"

"What, you gettin' fuckin' soft on me?"

"No, it's just that we don't even know if Sammy met up with her."

"Where the fuck else would he be? Sooner or later, his wife's gonna call around looking for him. You know how he's always checking in with her."

"On Friday nights? Forget about it, nobody calls their wife on Friday night, it's boys' night out."

"Sammy did. He really loves Sally, and when the boss finds out he's missing, we're gonna get whacked for it. You want that?"

"Fuck no, I'm just saying that maybe the wench don't know nothing."

"So what? It's just a few hours of work, then we dig a fuckin' hole. It ain't like we never whacked a wench before."

"What's wrong with you? You ever think before opening up that pie hole of yours? You make it sound like digging a hole is no big deal. You have any idea how rocky this fuckin' ground is up here in the mountains? It ain't like we're down at the Jersey shore."

I'd heard enough. I left my beer and walked over to the bar, where Debbie was still flirting with her friend at the other end. She looked over at me, then turned back to her friend for a few more seconds. Laughing it up, having a good old time.

She finally started heading over to me and her friend's eyes stayed glued to her ass as he licked his lips. She stopped to chat with about six more of her admirers, bending over before each one, elbows on the bar, using her cleavage as leverage to fatten her tip jar. She made it over to me and stood with her hands on her hips.

"Can I help you?"

"One more beer and then I'm going to head out."

She looked at me for a minute, a deadpan expression on her face, and walked over to the cooler in front of Bobby. She bent down and reached into the cooler, feeling around like she couldn't locate a mug, all the while flirting with Bobby. Now it was his turn to lick his lips. I should open up a Chapstick stand in this place, I'd make a fortune.

She finally pulled out a frosted mug and held it under the tap. She walked back over to me, placed it in front of me, no coaster, and walked away. It wasn't even a full glass, and the head was four inches thick. Fine. Be like that.

I sat down on my stool, determined not to look at Debbie for the rest of the night. Screw that bullshit. I had work to do and couldn't afford to be distracted.

I lasted four seconds before I caught myself staring at her again. Sheesh.

I needed to come up with a plan. What the hell was I going to do with these guys? How would I get them alone?

I thought Bobby's eyes were going to pop out of his head when she leaned over in front of him again.

*Focus!*

What if another of their "associates" was already on the way up here?

I could just wait in the bushes until they made a move on Mary Sue, but that was risky. I could miss them, or someone else might see me beating the hell out of them and tossing them in the bed of my truck for their final ride.

Out of the corner of my eye, I saw Fatty get out of his chair, pick up his beer, and walk towards me. He passed right by and headed to the men's room. With his beer? I guessed that he was the nontrusting type. Probably had to be that way to survive in his racket. Either that, or he'd been roofed before. The male rape scene from the movie *Deliverance* popped into my head and I couldn't help but chuckle.

Then all hell broke loose.

## 26

HER TIMING WAS IMPECCABLE, perfected over decades of daily practice. Fatty huffed his way down the bar, his tough guy chest stuck out, and Frances nailed him. I'm talking the grand pooh-bah of ass-grabbing finger probes that would have made a proctologist blush. Fat Boy jumped so high I thought he would hit his head on the smoke eater hanging from the ceiling. He didn't, but he did spill his beer all over his fancy shirt. I was laughing so hard I almost choked on mine.

One man's funny isn't necessarily another's. Fatty whipped around so fast, his arms extended, and whacked poor Frances in the shoulder, knocking her off her barstool and sending her rolling to the floor. He finished his violent pirouette with a profanity-laced rant that even Ralphie's dad would admire.

"Jesus fuckin' Christ, you stupid little cunt!"

The silence that followed was deafening. Everyone in the place stopped what they were doing. Beers were paused midway to mouths, kisses interrupted, the cook's finger hovered over the bell, Debbie stopped in midstride. Even the jukebox stopped. Every set of eyes in the place was daggered at Fatty. For a second the tension was so thick that my hand went to my Glock. I caught myself and pretend to scratch an itch in my side, looking down to conceal my smile. I'd seen the wrath of the Summit Savages before, and this was not going to be pretty.

Punches, kicks, elbows and beer bottles all rained down on Fatty as every patron in the place, except me of course, decided to teach the fat New York City asshole a lesson. Turned out that, despite all of Frances's faults, she had a lot of friends in Summit.

Some of the more humorous ones had even made a shield out of a cast-iron skillet. It had a big red sign on it that read "Frances's Skillet—100% Success Rate" and was meant to be tied around the rear of one's waist when you had to venture past her to use the restroom. It hung on the wall behind the bar, right next to the clock. Too bad Fatty didn't know enough to ask Debbie if he could use it.

While Debbie and Mary Sue helped Frances up and led her away from the melee, every one of her friends voiced their displeasure at Fatty and how he'd treated a long-upstanding citizen of Summit.

Now I knew better than anybody that we had our share of, let's just say, "imperfect" men, who'd done way worse than Fatty. But that didn't matter. They'd witnessed one of their own being abused in their house, and there was no tolerating that. Civic pride and all.

Within seconds, Fatty was on his hands and knees, trying to cover up and crawl away from the onslaught of what was now profanity-laced kicks to his ribs and thighs with sharp-toed cowboy boots.

But to no avail. All he succeeded in doing was giving the fellows who couldn't reach him a clean shot at him when he managed to crawl over to them.

I should have come to his aid, but no freakin' way was I stopping this show.

Skinny Boy had different ideas, and he came running over, swinging a chair to try and get the mob off the mobster. He was met with a blackjack from the off-duty corrections officer from the shock treatment facility. The same guy who had been sitting on *my* stool, trying to make time with *my* Debbie.

I had to admit, despite his puke-ugly face and portly body, he had good aim. Must have had a lot of practice. He nailed him dead center back of the head and dropped him like a sack of potatoes. Some of the patrons who hadn't had their lesson-teaching quota satisfied with Fatty, turned to Skinny Boy, and I felt like I was watching a replay.

I smiled, downed my beer, and ran out the door.

## 27

I FOUND their SUV in the parking lot and tried the door. It was unlocked. Jeez, this was perfect. I couldn't have orchestrated this any better if I'd had a ten-thousand-dollar budget and two months to plan it. I climbed in the backseat and looked out the tinted windows. The smell of the interior reminded me of Ostrich Boy.

A few minutes later I saw Fatty and Skinny being tossed into the parking lot, followed by cursing, some "don't ever come back here again," and a few more kicks for good measure. I felt a pride in my town that I hadn't known existed in me, and I couldn't help but grin as I lay down across the backseat and waited for Curly and Moe to go on their final ride.

It took ten or so minutes, but they finally made it close enough to the vehicle that I could hear their groaning and expletive-laced mumbling. I raised my head and peeked out the window a few times to check on their progress, and it was like watching paint dry. Skinny, the less injured of the two, was helping Fatty crawl across the gravel at a pace so slow that I started nodding off.

I was afraid that my body heat would fog the windows up and that they'd notice as they got closer. Not sure if they would put two and two together, even if they hadn't just had the shit kicked out of them, but there was nothing I could do about it anyway.

If they picked up on it and checked the backseat, I'd just have to beat them and slap the cuffs on. Part of me favored that scenario, and I had a mini-fantasy of grabbing them by their greasy slicked-back hair and slamming their foreheads together a couple of dozen times. But in the long run I'd have to put aside my selfish petty wants and just settle for killing them.

The passenger-side door was pulled open, and I felt the SUV sink to that side as Fatty tumbled into his seat. I could tell by the grunts that Skinny was doing all the work. He wasn't shy about telling us that, either.

"Jesus, you need to lose some weight. Fat fuck."

Fatty grunted an expletive in response. I couldn't make out all the words, him mumbling through broken teeth and all, but I was pretty sure that it was something about ball-licking.

The door slammed shut, and I heard Skinny Guy's footsteps on the gravel as he stumbled around the front of the SUV. I pulled out my Glock and screwed on the silencer. I prayed that I didn't have to use it yet, then realized that praying in a situation like this had limited value, so I laser-focused on the different scenarios if I was spotted in the backseat. I was nothing if not practical. Except when it came to Debbie. Damn her flirting! That's enough. Focus.

Skinny might be a neat freak and reach back to grab the paper towels to clean up Fatty's bloody drool. Then I had a decision to make. A head shot would be the easiest, but it would paint the windshield with his blood. That would suck. I wouldn't be able to drive without cleaning that mess up. I was sick and tired of cleaning shit up, I felt nauseous just thinking about it.

A back shot through the leather seat would work, unless I happen to clip something hard inside the seat, like a piece of the metal frame. I was confident that the nine-millimeter would brute-force its way into his back, but maybe it wouldn't do enough damage. He might cry like a baby and draw attention to his demise.

I could hear Fatty struggling to breathe through his nose, and he hadn't moved since he'd gotten in the SUV, so I figured he was out cold. I peeked around his seat and almost gasped when I saw him.

Holy crap, he looked like shit. He had a huge open gash on the bridge of his nose, another one over his eyes, which were already swollen shut, his nose was leaking blood all over his shirt, and his cheeks were so swollen that they looked like little aliens had burrowed under his skin and were setting up camp. And the worst of it, God help us all, his hair was messed up.

My creative mind already had "Summit Savages" T-shirts designed, complete with flying beer bottles and hammer fists as part of their logo, that I could hand out at the upcoming Red Barn Christmas party. As my present for everyone, I would have Debbie's T-shirt made up two sizes too small.

I sat up behind the driver's seat and slouched down as much as my muscular body would allow. I pointed my Glock at the seat back. Skinny pulled open the door and I heard voices. Shoot. I peeked out the window and saw a small mob, maybe four or five guys, leaving the Red Barn and trotting towards us.

Bobby and the shock camp corrections officer were in the lead, and Bobby had Frances's Skillet in his hand. This was not good. My mind went into negative overdrive. I found myself rooting for Skinny Boy to just shut up and drive away.

The voices got louder and grew into yells. "I thought we told you to get the fuck out of here."

Skinny Boy yelled back at them, "Fuck you, you redneck assholes," and slammed the door and started the SUV.

That was original.

I ducked back down in case they smashed the window. I heard loud banging and felt the big SUV shake from side to side. I knew that the savages were attacking. If they saw me in the backseat, my plan would be shot to hell.

An explosive sound came from the back of the vehicle, so loud that I jumped in my seat and then ducked for cover, hands over my head from instinct. Someone had shattered the back window.

Something rolled around on the floor and caught my attention. It was a ball from the pool table, and when it stopped spinning I could see that it was the eight ball.

*Now* these guys were getting out of control. I silently prayed that one of them didn't toss in a hand grenade. Those Summit guys could be pretty rough around the edges.

Skinny slammed the vehicle into drive and sped away from the mob. I could hear the loose parking lot gravel being kicked up by the spinning wheels and bouncing off the bottom of the vehicle.

Loud crashes banged off the sides and roof of the SUV, and I peeked out the back window and spotted Max and Gus throwing pool table balls at us. Wow, they really did love Frances.

Skinny Boy accelerated so fast on Route 10 that I felt like putting my seat belt on, but I couldn't risk him hearing the click. I gripped the seat so tight that my hands started to cramp up. Freakin' New York drivers...

He zoomed straight past the Sawyer Hill Road turnoff that would have taken us to the Lakeview House, and kept going on Route 10.

Shit. Where the hell was he going?

# 28

IT WAS VOYEURISTICALLY EERIE, sitting in the backseat behind the driver and listening to him mumble to himself. I fought the urge to grab his shoulder and scream *Boo!* in his ear at the top of my lungs while blasting a round from my Glock through the roof.

The only thing that stopped me was that he'd probably drive off the road and kill us all. Would've been funny as hell though.

After a few miles, the SUV slowed down to what I felt was a more appropriate speed, and I relaxed my death grip on my seat. I guessed that Skinny wanted to make sure no one was following, or that none of the savages from the Red Barn parking lot saw us turn off at Sawyer Hill Road. They might figure out they were staying at the Lakeview House and show up carrying pitchforks and torches.

He slowed the big SUV and turned off onto a back road, went a couple of hundred yards, and pulled over to the side.

I could hear him trying to catch his breath, to calm his nerves. He started with some feel-good affirmations but that didn't last. In no time, he was cursing everyone, including "the guy who founded this shit-eating little town." I liked our little town, and found his remarks offensive. He even stooped so low as to take the Lord's name in vain. Again.

I'd heard enough. I shot him three times in the back.

I leaned over to the front seat and whacked Fatty in the forehead with my pistol butt, just to make sure he stayed out cold. I hopped out of the SUV, dragged Skinny Guy from the front seat, tossed him in the second row and slammed the door closed. I took out the sanitizer-soaked towels from my Ziploc bag and cleaned the blood off the seat, then stuck the towels back in the Ziploc bag and in my pocket. I hopped in the front seat and took the back roads to Eminence.

I started to relax, feeling good about how the events of the night had played out. Even with the help of HFS, I couldn't have planned this any better. I'd tossed and turned for hours trying to figure out a way to get these two morons alone so that I could rid the earth of them, and all it had taken was a little finger probe from my new best friend Frances.

I vowed to always look back at her, smile and wink every time she grabbed my ass. In fact, I would go so far as to say that I promised the good Lord that I'd make additional trips to the men's room, just so Frances had something to look forward to and could keep her skills sharp, even if I didn't have to take a leak. Or I could just drink more beer, which would require more trips to the men's room. I liked that idea better.

My iPhone vibrated in my pocket, breaking me out of my fantasy. It scared the bejesus out of me, and I jumped so high that my head hit the ceiling. I pulled it out of my pocket, totally disregarding the no-texting-while-driving law. That sealed it, now I was *definitely* going to hell.

I looked at the screen and saw that it was from Debbie. I pulled over to the side of the road and read her text.

Debbie: You okay?

Me: Sure, you? *Of course I am*

Debbie: Yeah. Exciting, huh?

Me: Yeah. *You have no idea...*

Debbie: Sorry about last night.

Me: That's okay, me too. *Even though I didn't do anything wrong...*

Debbie: Love to see you tonight. Can I come over?

Me: I don't know, what did you have in mind? *Blowjob?*

Debbie: Making me beg, aren't you? Okay, fine, maybe I deserve it. I want you naked on the bearskin with Barry White and some merlot. Then I'm going to ravish you all night. Pretty please?

Me: Hmm...thinking... thinking. Well, alright, I guess so. *Hot damn freakin YEAH!*

Debbie: I'll text you when I leave.

Me: Roger. *Can't wait!*

God that felt good. It's amazing how good, and bad, a relationship can be for your mood. I was on cloud nine. Now I just had to get rid of Curly and Moe and I'd be back in good graces with my honey. I pulled the SUV out onto the road and raced towards Eminence.

It took me about half an hour to reach my property, then another twenty-five minutes on the tractor trail before reaching the well. I swung the big SUV wide, and backed up to the well. No use lugging these guys further than I had to. I turned off the vehicle, opened the door, and stepped out onto the grass. It felt good to get out of the SUV. Skinny Boy had shit his pants, so I had to drive the whole way with the freakin' windows open and it was cold.

I kept myself busy by calculating the wind-chill factor at the different speeds that I was driving. As an FYI, at forty miles per hour it was fifteen degrees.

I took out my phone and turned the flashlight on. I found the well right away, and my heart stopped.

The stone that covered it was off center, and it didn't line up with the indent in the surrounding soil that decades of gravity had created. I knew that I lined it up perfectly when I replaced it.

Holy shit.

That meant that Ostrich Boy had lived through the toss into the well, the bullets that I'd wasted on him, and the two big rocks that I'd thrown down after him. And climbed out! This was bad.

I moved the light around to look for tracks, but didn't see any. He could be anywhere, even right behind me. I turned and searched the nearby shrubs with my flashlight, but I didn't see him.

I had to work fast. I bent down and slid the stone all the way off. I dragged Skinny Guy from the backseat and, unable to control my anger, I smacked him in the face. Then I tossed him down the well. I opened the driver's-side door, undid Fatty's seat belt, and dragged him over to the well. Skinny was right, he weighed a freaking ton. I hoped he'd fit down the well and not get stuck halfway down. That could be awkward.

He started moving, and with Ostrich Boy running in the wild there was no time for pleasantries. I took out my Glock and shot him in the chest two times, then rolled him into the well before he had a chance to bleed all over the place. I know it was selfish of me, but I was so tired of cleaning up blood. I kicked the two empty shells in after him, the pleasant echo of brass tinkling off the rocks music to my ears.

I opened the Ziploc bag and tossed it in the well. I pushed the stone back over it. I'd have to come back here soon with my backhoe to fill the well up with dirt. Maybe I'd locate Ostrich Boy by then and I could reacquaint him with his buddies.

That brought up an interesting quandary. Would he have been able to make it through the night? He had to be injured from the fall in the well, and I knew he was soaked to the bone. The temps last night had hit a low of twenty-two degrees, so unless he'd managed to build a fire, he would have frozen.

If he had lived through the night, would he even have been able to find his way out of here? That was no easy task. We were in the middle of a gazillion-acre forest, and I could have been wrong, but I couldn't picture Ostrich Boy as being that backwoods savvy.

Then it hit me. I smacked my forehead and groaned. Holy crap, I should have believed my eyes when I'd thought I'd seen him ball up when I'd tossed him down the well. He had been conscious, and that was how he'd made it out of the well! I chastised myself for underestimating him. I would not make that mistake again.

I had to get rid of the SUV, so on the way down the tractor trail I stopped at one of my large barns and retrieved my motorbike. I threw it into the back of the SUV and climbed in the driver's seat.

My tractor trail intersected my driveway right where it met the East Road. It wasn't really a road; it was nothing more than a single-lane dirt path through the forest. Instead of making a right turn and heading down to Summit, I made a left and continued deeper into the woods. About halfway down to West Kill Road, I made a right onto an access trail. Access trails are paths that are cleared through the forest so that the lumber harvesters can haul out their goods. They don't even qualify as dirt roads, since they're lined with old pine needles and littered with tree stumps.

I went to the end of the trail and made my own trail deeper into the woods—no easy feat in the dark. After I'd gone as far as possible, I opened every window, the sunroof, all the doors, and even the hood. I killed the engine for the last time and removed my motorbike from the rear of the vehicle. I wiped the interior down with some of the sanitized paper towels I'd saved from my Ziploc bag. I punctured all four tires with my Swiss Army knife and ripped out some engine wires for good measure.

This section of state land had been logged recently, and wasn't scheduled to be logged again for another seventeen years, so the odds of someone finding the vehicle were slim to none. With all doors and windows opened, I estimated that nature would wipe clean the interior in a few weeks, and any traces of my DNA that I might have missed with my wipe-down would be gone forever.

I took one last look at the hulking machine. It looked so out-of-place, every opening opened and sitting in the dark forest. The interior lights were still on, and the door chimes still tried to tell its moron driver that the doors were open.

I climbed on my motorbike, started her up, and made my way back to East Road. I was relieved to be rid of the open door chimes that would probably go on for days. I felt a sudden sense of pity for all the animals that had to put up with that. I vowed to myself that next time I'd remember to bring a wrench to disconnect the battery.

I took the less traveled roads back to Summit to avoid being seen. Except for the unknown about Sam's existence,

I was happy with the way that things had worked out. The more I thought about it, the more I convinced myself that Sam was dead, lying frozen somewhere in the deep woods.

When I got to my truck, I saw that Debbie's car was gone. I wondered if she'd spotted mine. That could lead to some awkward questions. Hopefully she was so excited to get to my place that she hadn't noticed it.

I threw the motorbike in the back of my pickup and took off for Eminence.

I texted Debbie, while driving, and she replied that she was almost there and there was no way I was getting out of pleasing her *all* night, so I'd better bring my A game.

I smiled to myself.

## 29

When Sam woke up, his fire was almost out and it was already dark out. He'd slept a little longer than he'd planned, but at least his clothes were dry and he was warm except for his feet. As cool and hip as his two-thousand-dollar pair of boots made him feel, they didn't do shit to keep his feet warm.

His plan to retrace his way back to the well and then down the trail might have to be put on hold. The moonlight provided some light, and the light layer of snow made it a little easier to see, but he had mixed feelings about trying to travel in the dark. What if he got lost?

He stood up and stretched his arms over his head, pleasantly surprised that he wasn't sore from sleeping on the ground. He studied the surrounding landscape. It was vital that he be sure about which direction to go before he moved from his base. He knew from his Boy Scout days that starting off in the wrong direction in the middle of the forest would be a disaster, and silently thanked his scout-master for driving into him the importance of visually marking landmarks as he traveled through the woods.

He recognized the closer landmarks, but had a moment of doubt because everything looked different at night. He mulled over his options for a few minutes and decided that he would get the hell out of here. He took a deep breath and started walking. This was it.

Within a few minutes, he spotted the next landmark and continued acquiring and following landmarks until he came upon the clearing around the well. A sense of relief swept over him. He was home free now, and he felt like singing when he picked up the tractor trail that had brought him here. He followed the trail.

He'd had plenty to think about in the hours he'd walked down the trail, and for the first time in his adult life, he started to second-guess his life choices. Nearly dying in a well and seeing Sally and their daughter Barbara without him had struck a nerve. Perhaps he was getting soft in his old age. Maybe this life wasn't for him anymore.

He had millions stashed away in a safe deposit box. Why not give up the life and settle down? Everyone knew that you couldn't just leave the life, but he could go off grid, change his name, relocate somewhere in rural America or even Mexico. Nobody would ever find him, and he could live a peaceful life, not looking over his shoulder every second for someone to put a bullet in him.

Sure, Sally and Barbara would have to give up their friends, but most of them were phonies anyway. Would they go for it? They'd talk in few days. Right now, he needed to kill the bastard who'd tossed him in the well, grab his buddies, and get the hell out of this shit hole.

There were plenty of divots and rocks on the trail to navigate around, and his progress was slower than he'd thought it'd be. His feet were cold, but the rest of him was warm because of the workout. He'd developed a nice steady rhythm to his slow pace, stepping fast enough to stay warm but not so fast that he started sweating or risked losing his footing on the trail's imperfections.

He rounded a bend in the trail and there it was. A house. It looked like some kind of A-frame log cabin and had a winding driveway that led to a two-car garage. He followed the trail down to where it intersected the front of the driveway. The person who'd dumped him in the well must live here. Nobody would dump a body down someone else's well. Right?

He felt his adrenaline pick up and he envisioned emptying his Derringer into the back of the guy's head. He'd teach that bastard.

He crouched down next to an evergreen and looked around for signs of life. There were faint tire tracks that led up the driveway to the garage, but no car. Maybe it was in the garage? There were no lights on in the house, and he didn't hear anything. He stood up and walked along the tree line towards the house.

After a few steps he picked up a sound, barely audible, but getting louder. It was a car approaching. He ducked back into the woods and turned towards the road, where he spotted approaching headlights. Hopefully it would pass right by the driveway, but this place was so out-of-the-way, he couldn't imagine them passing by. He reached into his pocket and felt the Derringer. Thank God for that.

He watched the car as it approached the driveway entrance and saw the reflective glow of the brake lights when the car slowed. Fuck. It turned into the driveway.

He crouched by an evergreen and watched as the car approached. It moved slow, overly cautious on the slick gravel. Right before it reached his position he jumped out in front of it, pistol aimed at the driver's head. *"Stop! Fuckin' stop!"*

The car braked to a halt, and he held the gun on the driver as he opened the passenger door and slid in.

His surprise was evident in the tone of his voice. "Holy shit, it's you?"

---

## 30

HE WAVED the gun towards the house. "Drive, bitch."

She took her foot off the brake and pulled up the drive-way. "Please don't shoot me." Her voice quivered like a scared little girl.

"Shut the fuck up. You only talk when I ask you something. Understand me?" She nodded.

He pointed to the house. "You live here?"

"No. Just visiting." She pulled the BMW in front of the garage door and killed the engine.

"Who lives here?"

"Jack Lamburt."

"What's he do?"

"Sheriff."

"Describe him to me."

"Tall, fair skin, short hair, athletic."

Sam grinned and his pulse quickened when she

described the guy from that wench waitress's house. Sheriff, eh? No wonder the douchebag didn't know how to get rid of a body. Didn't have the balls to shoot someone in cold blood. Well, he did.

"Get out." He exited the BMW and followed her up the front steps, the little Derringer pressed against her lower back. They reached the front door and she went to punch in the keypad code to unlock the door. Sam grabbed her elbow. "Wait. Anybody home?"

"No."

"Any alarms in the house?"

"No."

"Okay, open the door slow, and no funny stuff or I shoot. Got it?"

"Yes."

"Good. Now nice and slow." He held the gun tight against her. "We're gonna have a little party while we wait for your sheriff friend, and I like my women without any bullet holes, so don't make me shoot you."

Debbie punched in the code and pushed open the front door. She stepped inside and turned on the light.

Sam looked around. "Nice pad." He raised his hand and smacked Debbie across the face, knocking her to the hard-wood floor.

The big dog tore across the room and leapt at Sam's throat. His jaws closed on the meaty flesh, and the two of them fell backwards into the door frame and slid down to the floor with a thud.

The dog held his grip on Sam's throat, not so tight as to kill him, just tight enough to keep him pinned on the floor against the wall. Cold fear spread through him and the pain of the dog's teeth in his neck froze him in place.

Sam fumbled around for the little Derringer he'd dropped, found it, and fired both of its rounds. The dog yelped, released Sam's throat, and limped out the front door, whimpers of pain coming from him.

"Jesus fuckin' Christ, that dog's a fuckin' beast." Sammy moved on his knees and slammed the front door closed. "He almost took my head off." He felt his neck for blood.

He walked over to Debbie and smacked her in the face again. "Why didn't you warn me?" His whole body was shaking from anger, his face beet-red. "That dog could've killed me," he screamed at her.

Debbie sat there on the floor, her hands covering her face, crying. "I'm sorry, I'm sorry."

Sam grabbed a handful of her hair, pulled her over to the bearskin rug, and threw her down. He stood over her and smiled, and he heard her smartphone vibrate in her pocket.

"Gimme that." He held his hand out.

Debbie reached into her pocket, took out her phone, and gave it to him with a shaky hand. Sammy read the text and laughed.

"Hot stud? Who the fuck is 'hot stud'?"

Between sobs, Debbie managed to squeak out a reply. "Jack."

"Oh. Nice, he says he'll be here in half an hour." He smiled as he gave her the news. He looked down at the phone, thumbed out a text, and hit send. "Perfect timing, now take off your clothes. I'm going to show you what a hot stud is."

# 31

DEBBIE LOOKED UP AT HIM, crossed her arms over her chest, and offered feigned resistance. "No." After the conversation at the bar and seeing his actions tonight, she had him pegged for what he was. An insecure little man. Napoleon complex to a T. And she knew just how to play him.

"You bitch." He reared back and slapped her in the face again. She fell backwards onto the rug, and he leaned over and tore her shirt off in one violent motion. He gawked at her near nakedness like a wide-eyed teen witnessing his first porn. He took off his belt and tied it around Debbie's wrists, then raised them over her head and attached the other end of the belt to a leg of the couch.

She closed her eyes and thought of being tied up and taken by Jack, a vision that, no matter where she was or what she was doing, always aroused her. She felt her nipples tighten. *Good, that'll get his attention.*

He reached down with both hands, slid them under her bra, and lifted it up and over her breasts, letting it rest around her neck. He exhaled with a hoot. "Woo-hoo! Holy shit, look at those tits. And those fuckin' nipples! Halle-fuckin'-lujah." He rubbed his palms together like a little kid on Christmas morning who was about to tear open his first present.

He grabbed her ankles and pulled her towards the fire-place, never taking his eyes off of her chest. Her arms were extended straight overhead. He let her legs fall and removed her high heels, fondling and smelling them before tossing them aside. "Nice shoes. You have good taste for a bartender."

He spotted a bottle of red wine on the end table next to an iPad that was all set up to play music. He tapped the play icon, and the low sultriness of Barry White's "What Am I Gonna Do With You" serenaded them.

He grabbed the wine bottle, popped the cork, filled the two glasses, and did a little two-step to the music. He raised a glass for a toast and downed it.

"To us. A match made in heaven."

*What a bozo.* It took all of her strength not to laugh out loud.

He reached down and opened her jeans, and slid them off her legs. He stood and stared, his eyes laser-focused on her sheer thong, his chin resting on his chest, and his voice came out in a whisper that was barely audible. "Oh my God.

You are fuckin' beautiful. Beautiful." He looked upwards and did the sign of the cross. "Thank you, God."

He knelt down between her legs and slipped a finger under the top of her panties to slide them down. "Up," he said in a soft voice, motioning to her hips. She raised her butt just enough for him to slide the panties past her hips and down both legs.

He coddled her panties with both hands, like a newborn baby. He brought them up to his nose and inhaled so deep that Debbie thought he might get dizzy and fall over. He exhaled, eyes closed, with a delirious smile so wide that Debbie knew she had him.

"Please. Stop," she said, her voice nothing more than a whimper.

"Oh, man, you are so sweet." He pushed her knees open, leaned forward, and kissed her stomach just below her belly button.

Debbie forced a full-body quiver, then moaned. "Please. Don't do that."

He looked up from between her legs. "Oh, you like that, don't you?"

"No. Stop."

He kissed his way down to the top of her pubic hair, and ran his tongue across the top of it. Her fake moan was louder this time. "Oh God... stop."

He lay down on his stomach and ran both arms under her thighs, clasping his hands down on her hips. He shouldered her thighs up, and she rested them against his ears with her calves on his back. He licked his way down until her moist flesh parted under his tongue. Her breath caught in her throat, and she groaned an unconvincing "Oh God no... Stop. Please."

He chuckled. "You love this, don't you? You slut. I knew it."

"No. Not at all. Stop." She flung her head from side to side and pretended to try and squirm away, but she only succeeded in raising her hips up to his chin. She felt his hands clamp tighter around her hips. "No," she whimpered.

He buried his face between her legs and she reacted by tightening her thighs against his ears. She moaned out loud. "Oh God, yes!" *I've got you now.*

She writhed and moaned, taking short, quick breaths. "Oh God. You're so good." *And stupid as shit.*

She lowered her left leg to the floor and rested it lightly on his right forearm. "Pinch my nipples... Please." *And seal your fate.*

He slid his right arm from under her leg and up her stomach. He grabbed a handful of her breast and squeezed hard. "Yes, that's it." She bucked against him, luring him deeper into her jiu jitsu web. One arm in, one arm out.

She moaned, begging him to continue. "God, that feels so good." *Almost as good as killing you is going to feel.*

The first wave of her fake orgasm barreled over the horizon and she bucked and moaned between gritted teeth. "Just a little more." *And you're as good as dead.*

She slid her right calf up higher on his back until her

ankle was resting on the back of his right shoulder. She lifted her left leg, placed the back of her knee across the top of her right ankle, and rested her left calf on his back.

*Few more seconds...*

She continued to buck and shake in her fake orgasm, and moaned loud to distract him as she inched her upper body to the right to get a better angle. She slid her left calf off of his back and quickly folded her leg down over her right ankle, and locked in the triangle choke.

Poor Sam got caught with one arm in, one arm out, a definite no-no in jiu jitsu. She brought her thighs together so tight that he gasped and his whole body froze. His face still buried against her, he tried to raise his head, but the triangle choke was locked in so deep and strong that he couldn't move.

He raised his eyes to look up at her. She smirked down at him, a calm blackness replacing the feigned pleasure in her eyes.

"Oh, honey," she whispered. "Please don't stop now." She squeezed a little tighter, then released a little pressure, playing with him like a shark tossing a baby seal in the air.

With his free hand he fumbled around on the floor, grabbed his Derringer, and pointed it at her face.

She laughed at him. She'd known the second she'd seen him point the little pistol at her that it was a two-shot .22-caliber Derringer. She even owned three of them herself, one with a very ladylike pink grip. After firing twice at London, the gun was empty. Sam pulled the trigger.

"It's empty, you moron." She chuckled and gave in to her sadistic side. "You shouldn't have shot your load on a dog."

She knew from locking in thousands of triangle chokes on her fellow jiujitsu students in over a decade of practice, that it was over. She saw the same realization in his eyes, right before they rolled up into his forehead, and she smiled.

The front door crashed open.

## 32

I SUSPECTED something was wrong when Debbie replied to my texts using one only word answers. She had two traits that mildly annoyed me: she was fiery as heck, and she could be a talker. Sometimes, especially after a few glasses of wine and before I satisfied her, she could go on about things long after the point was made. Good egg that I am, I tolerated it. It wasn't like she was an axe murderer or anything, and as annoying as her few flaws were, her good traits way outnumbered them.

One of my "bad" traits, according to her, was that I was paranoid. I tended to think a better word was "careful," but she wasn't buying that, so I'd agreed that I'd work on my "paranoia."

Just the same, tonight I was going to be a little careful, so I pulled my truck into one of the forest access trails that was close to my driveway. In the name of stealth, I intended to go it on foot from here.

I pulled my pickup around a bend in the trail so that it wouldn't be visible from the road. In my business you always covered your tracks, even in the darkness of night, if you wanted to stay alive. And out of jail. Just being "careful."

I killed the engine, stepped out onto the pine needles and soft closed the door. The forest always smelled so good to me. Pine and other green scents, mixed with a hint of dampness. I inhaled and soaked in the pleasant smell of nature that hadn't changed at all since I was a kid. Good memories.

I took out my phone and turned the ringer off. My eyes had adjusted to the moonlight, and I could see the trail well enough without the need for my iPhone flashlight, so I stuffed it back in my pocket.

I trotted towards the road, my footsteps silent on the bed of soft pine needles, my breathing quiet. I heard nothing other than a soft breeze filtering through the treetops. A good sign.

I reached the gravel road that borders my acreage in a few minutes, and stepped up and over the small rock wall that surrounded my property. The ground is so rocky here that the first thing the Dutch settlers did when they arrived in the late 1700s was clear the fields of them so they could grow food. Some of the rocks were stacked up to form two-foot-thick basement or foundation walls for the new homes the settlers were building.

The others were used to create a stone wall perimeter fence that was around two feet high and a foot and a half wide at the base. My two hundred plus acres had been in my family for over a century, and with so many vacations and summer breaks spent in Eminence, I knew these stone walls like the back of my hand.

Most of our acreage was wooded, and our house was located in a big clearing that was set back from the road about two hundred feet. The driveway was gravel with a slight curve, but I wouldn't be using that tonight.

I crept between the trees, still listening hard for anything out-of-place, and heard nothing. Everything was as it should be. But I knew better. I knew something was wrong.

The wooded area around the front of my house was thinned out, but not cleared. Most of the trees were ever-green, but we still had quite a few hardwoods. The leaves they shed every fall were much crunchier than the fragile pine needles that coated the forest trail, and I had to step slow and soft to minimize the crunching sound that came with each step.

I worked my way up to the clearing that was around my A-frame log cabin and spotted Debbie's BMW in my drive-way. It was parked in front of the right-side garage door. In my spot. Me being a swell guy and all, I let her park in front of the left side garage door because it's closest to the house.

She never parked in my spot. The fact that something

was wrong couldn't have been clearer to me if she'd held up a neon sign. Good girl. I took out my Glock.

My fears about Sam were coming true before my eyes. I chastised myself again for not ensuring that the douche was dead, but then I focused on the task at hand. The fact the Debbie's "something is wrong" signal of parking her BMW in my spot meant that someone, likely Sam, had been in her car. Otherwise she wouldn't have known to park in my spot to alert me. But how had he managed to do that?

The most likely scenario was an armed carjack, but if this was the work of Sam, where had he gotten a gun from? All my guns were locked away in safes, so even if he'd broken into my house before Debbie arrived, he wouldn't have gotten any of my guns. Plus, she wouldn't have known to park in my spot unless he was in her car. Had he had a second firearm on him at Mary Sue's house? If so, how did I miss it?

And where was London? I instinctively looked over to my hammock and saw the outline of a mound in the grass. Right where he always fell asleep and waited for me. Except this time he didn't greet me. He didn't even move. Oh no. It hit me like a freight train.

London was hurt bad, or even dead.

I resisted the urge to go over and confirm it, but there was no way that he was okay. A ghost couldn't come on our property without him noticing it and trotting over to check out the potential invader, which was usually a chipmunk or rabbit. "Perimeter secure, London?" was probably the most frequently spoken phrase I've ever said in my life.

But I would probably say it no more.

I'm not an emotional guy, but London was such a great friend, especially to Cheryl. God she loved that dog. I'd never forget the first time I went over to her condo in Princeton. She opened the door to let me in and the first thing I saw, after her lovely smile, was London sitting by her side. He didn't bark or growl, he just sat there with his ears up and watched me.

The whole night.

Cheryl made this fantastic steak dinner, and when we finished and moved to her couch to watch a movie, he followed. He was respectful and kept his distance, but I was never out of his sight.

It took a while, but eventually he and I bonded and he relinquished the role of alpha male of the house to me. I thought about how he was one of my last attachments to Cheryl, and my eyes watered up.

He must have been wounded, most likely shot, and gone to the one place above all others that he found comfort in. By my side at the hammock. Except I wasn't there for him.

I no longer had to assume the worst. I knew it for sure. An armed attacker was holding Debbie hostage inside my house. Or, she was already dead. I took a few breaths to get control of my anger, took one last look at London, and stepped closer to the house.

I approached from the left, made it to the corner, and

slid along the front to look in the living room picture
window. This was the second time in two nights I'd Peeping
Tommed it, and I was already good at it. If this sheriff thing
didn't work out, I could always make a killing selling
Peeping Tom videos online.

I reached the lower corner of the window and listened
for any sign of life before looking in. I didn't hear anything.
I raised my head and looked in the window.

There was a fire in the fireplace and two glasses of red
wine on an end table. The lights were dimmed, and I could
hear the sexy bass rhythm of Barry White's "My First, My
Last, My Everything," a song that we'd danced to so many
times that just hearing a stranger hum it on line at Star-
bucks brought thoughts of Debbie and me locked in an intimate embrace.

My heart nearly stopped when I saw two writhing
bodies on my bearskin rug. *What the?*

Holy Fuck. My Debbie? She was on her back, and even
with the dim light I could tell that she was naked. Ostrich
Boy was between her legs.

And God help me, she was smiling!

## 33

In slow motion, I saw Ostrich Boy raise a hand and point it towards Debbie's face. I caught a glint of light reflecting from his hand and regained my focus. It was a gun. I almost crapped in my pants.

I raced to the front door and smashed it open, entering the living room just as I heard the click of a dry-firing pistol. The gun was empty.

Debbie looked up at me, down at Ostrich Boy, and blurted out; "I swear, honey, this isn't what it looks like…"

God I loved her sense of humor. She looked back down at Ostrich Boy's reddening forehead, grunted, and squeezed her legs together so tight that he dropped his pistol and his whole body went limp. Out cold.

I was in awe. "Holy shit, where'd you learn to do that?"

She smiled, but didn't answer me.

I got on my knees and untied her. She reached up, put

her arms around my neck, pulled me down and kissed me right on the lips. I thought I was going to lose my balance, so I put my hand out to brace myself, and it landed on her breast. Purely accidental, I swear.

She stopped kissing me, and I thought she was going to chastise me for feeling her up at a totally inappropriate time. She gestured down to Ostrich Boy, his red forehead still locked tight between her legs, looking like a plump tomato ready to burst.

"I'm okay with how you can't control yourself with Barry playing in the background and all, but this is a little too kinky even for me. Perhaps you can properly dispose of douchebag, and we can pick up where we left off?"

## 34

---

"HHMMₚₚғғ. HHMMPPFFHH!"

My passenger woke up and tried to speak. I looked over at him and shook my head in disgust. *Shithead.*

I reached out and ripped the duct tape from his mouth so hard I left a bright red rectangle on his face. I balled the tape up and tossed it out the window.

"*Fuck!*" he screamed and leaned forward in pain. "Do you know who I am?"

"Yeah, yeah, yeah, save it, dipshit."

"You're a dead man, do you hear me, a fucking dead man. Nobody does this to Big Sam and lives to talk about it." He pulled at the handcuffs which I'd chained and padlocked around his size-forty-something waist.

I nodded to his lap. "Having some trouble there, Fat Sam? That chain can hold fifteen thousand pounds, so don't even bother."

"You're the one with fuckin' trouble. I don't know who you think you are, but I know that you're a dead man. A *fuckin' dead man!*" Spittle flew from his mouth, and he yanked violently at the chains, left and right, up and down, like a rabid animal snared in a trap who could smell the hunter closing in on him for the kill.

"Easy there, chubby, you don't want to hurt yourself."

"Fuck you, you piece of dog shit." Drool came out of his mouth, and his face was so beet-red from anger that the red rectangle around his mouth blended in with the rest of his face.

I was afraid he might have a stroke, so I took out my blackjack and whacked him in the forehead, careful not to hit his nose so he wouldn't bleed all over my interior. The last thing I needed was to clean up another goddam mess. As it was, it'd probably take me a good twenty minutes to contain and clean up the oil slick his hair had left on his seat.

I looked over at him and shook my head in disbelief. What a freakin' bastard. After all he'd been through, his hair was still perfect. I felt like hitting him again, but held off.

My blackjack shot to his forehead wasn't forceful enough to knock him out, but it stunned him enough that he just sat there in a silent daze for a few minutes. I sighed and relaxed. Finally, some peace and quiet.

It was a clear night, so I dimmed the dashboard lights down and leaned forward to glance up through the windshield. The night sky was filled with stars. There were millions of them, and I could even see the Milky Way. It was so close it looked fake, like being at a planetarium. It always amazed me how clear the night became once you escaped from the air and light pollution of the big cities.

A few minutes later, my peace and quiet was interrupted by childlike sniffling coming from my passenger. Oh well, the silence had been great while it'd lasted.

I looked over, cursed him again for his hair, and saw tears streaming down his chubby cheeks mixing with snot from his nose before bubbling up at his lips. There was a big red lump on his forehead where my blackjack had kissed him. It matched the red rectangle around his mouth.

For a second I almost felt sorry for him. Then I thought of all the HFS intel I'd gathered on him and what he'd done to Debbie and Mary Sue. And London.

I felt like hitting him again. The only reason I didn't was because I'd been up for so long that I was way beyond fatigued, and I didn't trust my aim. Missing his nose and avoiding a blood fest with two shots in a row in a moving vehicle would be pushing my luck. A man's got to know his limitations.

"Why? What have I ever done to you?" He sounded contrite now, but he couldn't fool me. I'd been following him through HFS for more than two years. I knew more about Sam and his family than Sam did. Not just the criminal enterprises he ran, but his personal life too.

HFS had every eavesdropping hardware imaginable in

his house. We called it "Sammy's Smarthouse," SS for short. Every single room of his six-thousand-plus-square-foot house had multiple smart home devices, each one hacked and turned into our personal wiretap and pinhole video camera. I had a front-row seat to one of the most violent criminal enterprises ever to hit the East Coast. Sam had his greedy little fingers in anything that made him money, from heroin to small arms, to pimping little kids—he sold it all. He ran his empire like a little Napoleon, and at last count he had twenty eight dead bodies to his credit. And most painful of all, one dog.

To top it all off, he was a selfish lover.

Karma was a bitch, and it was time for Sam to get his dose. I looked over at him and smiled.

"I'm fucking Sally tonight," I said.

"What? Yeah, you wish."

"No, seriously. You know when she goes to yoga on Sunday evenings? Where you have your simpletons follow her to make sure that she's being a 'good girl'?"

"They follow her to make sure she's safe, you moron. Hey...wait a minute...how'd you know about that?"

I laughed. "Yeah, sure they do. Well, she walks in the front door and runs right out the back door and into my van. She's naked in under thirty seconds. We drive around to the front, park next to your dumbass hammerheads in their Chevy SUV, and while you think your wife's in yoga, stretching and sweating, she's riding me like a coked-up whore."

He smirked a dismissal. "What's wrong with you? You're sick. You think I believe that horseshit?"

"And that mole under her left breast that you always made fun of? Well, I happen to love it."

I kept looking straight out the windshield, and I could see him staring at me through my peripheral vision. I paused for a minute before continuing to give his walnut-sized brain time to think. Then I delivered the dagger;

"You know that thing that she does with her tongue under your balls, where she strokes your cock and buries her face in your nuts while she plays with herself until she comes? Well, she does that with me too. Except, she really comes, none of this pretend stuff like she does with you." I stuck out my chest like a proud father after his kid hit a walk-off home run in the T-ball World Series.

"Ain't that freakin' awesome?" I looked over at him and raised an open hand. "High five, bro!" I frowned and looked down at the handcuffs. "Oh—that's right, you can't."

I delivered the second dagger;

"Anyway, two weeks ago, she rode me with my cock up her ass." I glanced down at my crotch with a raised eyebrow, then smirked at him. "No easy feat, if you get my drift." I nudged him with my elbow.

He looked straight ahead and shook his head side to side. "No way."

"Swear to God, no shit. Don't believe me? Come on, you remember that night. She came home and you asked her why she was limping? She told you she stretched too hard during class and must have pulled a muscle. You were like, "No more of that yogi bullshit for you." Remember that? I laughed for like ten minutes when she told me that. Yogi. Sheesh."

I let that sink on for awhile, and continued;

"Anyway, I know you don't go that way with her, but she loved it, man. You should have seen her face, you would have been so proud." I paused again for theatrical effect. Minutes went by before he broke our silence with a series of head shakes.

"No. No. No. You lie." His voice was low and lacked feeling, like he was in a drug-induced daze. "Not my Sally. She would never do that to me."

"Yeah, your Sally. Who do you think hired me?"

"No. *No!* You lie. Shut up, you bastard!" He pulled against his chains and kicked out with his feet. "Fuck you, you lying bastard." He stared at me, eyes glaring daggers, and spat on my face.

I whacked him with my blackjack. Damn my impulse control issues. Just when I thought I had it under control, I went and did something risky.

Like most things in life, we tended to overanalyze and think too much about even the simplest of details. I nailed him in the same exact spot on his forehead. So much for worrying about fatigue throwing off my aim.

A few minutes later he came around, and I continued my made-up mental assault. "You know that four million dollars in cash in your safe deposit box at Wells Fargo on Livermore Street? Her and I are splitting it. Fifty-fifty, pal."

Sammy looked straight ahead and his body started to quiver. My words were taking its toll on the tough guy mobster. The shit I was spewing was all gathered from HFS surveillance, so that part of it was true. With that part being accurate, it only made sense that he'd believe everything that I said. After all, how would I know all of those things unless Sally had told me?

He slouched in his seat and cried like a little girl who'd witnessed her new kitten flattened by an eighteen-wheeler. I continued.

"Oh, and by the way, your daughter's next, Sammy. Did I mention that I'm one of Barbara's mentors at Penn State? Yeah, baby, nothing like a little freshman meat to make an old guy feel young again." Now I really stuck my chest out. "I can't wait to hit that. *Yummy!* I'm just glad she looks like her mom, and not you." I laughed.

"Why?" he asked. His voice so low that I had trouble hearing him.

I leaned towards him and cupped my ear. "Eh? Come again?"

"Why are you doing this?"

"Why? Shit, Sam, I've been spying on your fat ass for over two years now. I've seen all the shit that you've done, the drugs that you sold, the young girls you pimped, the guys you killed. I've seen it all. But I'm HFS, and HFS doesn't care about anything but terrorism. And since you're not a terrorist, they just turn all that shit that I accumulated on you over to the FBI, and forget about you. But since HFS's domestic spying is illegal, the FBI's hands where tied.

But I couldn't forget about you, and my hands aren't tied. Once your cell phone signal got within one hundred miles of me, the fun started. I couldn't believe how lucky I was. You visiting my little out-of-the-way town. I usually have to hunt down the shitheads that I kill. But not you. You fell right into my lap. Thanks for making it easy for me."

"That's it? No. Wait, please, I'm really not like that. You have to understand, I can't run a business without being tough as nails." He sniffled, then stifled a cough as he explained what he meant. "We live in a brutal world. If those thugs, those street criminals, if they see that you're soft, they'll be all over you." He wiped his runny nose on his shoulder. "A man's got to earn respect in this business, and sometimes you have to earn that respect the tough way." He looked at me to see if he'd scored any points.

I didn't acknowledge him, and he must have taken my silence as a sign that he was winning me over, so he went on.

"You know, you got some big balls, fella. I could use a guy like you in my operation. We could work things out between us, no hard feelings, and you'd be in for some big paydays. I don't know what those KFC dicks pay you, but I can triple it, no problem." He smiled again, this time a little wider, trying hard to win me over.

"You killed my dog."

"What? Oh, that. You can't blame me for that. I mean, come on, what a fuckin' beast that dog was," he laughed. "My life flashed before my eyes. I thought I was gonna crap in my pants. If you're half as brave as him, you'll fit in with my crew just fine. Besides, he was just a dog. You know they eat dogs in China, right?"

What an ass. I couldn't show any emotion and give him the satisfaction of getting to me.

I cleared my throat and composed myself.

"It's too bad. Sally was really attached to London. She's gonna be very upset when I tell her that you killed him."

His mouth opened and I could see him staring at me through the corner of my eye. I ignored him. *Shithead.*

I checked my GPS for the third time to confirm that we were on the east side of Jeffrey's Ledge.

"We. Are. Heeere!" I announced, doing my best to sound like an MMA announcer. I looked over at Big Sam and laughed. The wrinkled forehead look of confusion on his face was priceless. I wanted to snap a photo and post it on Facebook so bad, but for once, I was successful in controlling my impulses.

"Here? What the hell you talking about, here? We're in the middle of fucking nowhere." He turned in his seat and looked all around us. "I can't even see a light anywhere."

I reached over, undid his seat belt, and unlocked his door.

"What are you doing? What the fuck are you doing?"

The panic in his crackling voice rose with each word and reached an octave that I'd never heard from a post-pubescent male. So much for the tough guy mobster lore.

"I'll tell Sally you said hi." I turned the yoke hard to the right, and the little Cessna went into a steep bank. I placed my hand on his hip and helped "Big Sam" slide out the door, his greasy hair an unexpected aid to his exit. Good riddance.

Even over the roar of the three-hundred horsepower engine, I could hear him screaming on his way down to the Atlantic Ocean.

I leveled off the small plane, leaned over, and pulled his door shut. I shivered and goose bumps rose on my neck. Holy crap, it was freaking cold at this altitude. I looked up at my outside air temperature gauge that hung on the top of my windshield next to my compass and saw that it was in the low teens.

Did I mention that I love math? I mentally calculated the wind-chill factor for a falling body, which is $35.74 + 0.6215T - 35.75V \wedge 0.16 + 0.4275TaV \times 0.16$.

Wow. Minus twenty degrees Fahrenheit. Holy shit, that's cold!

No wonder he was screaming.

To give the radar watchers at the air traffic control room an appearance of a normal flight, I continued flying south along Victor 167, a highway in the sky that runs from Maine to Cape Code, for another fifteen miles before punching in the GPS coordinates to my home airport and turning westbound.

I climbed up to four thousand five hundred feet, which was an appropriate altitude for west bound flight, and engaged the autopilot. I reached behind me and grabbed my thermos of coffee that Debbie had made me. She always made the best coffee, and even after a couple of hours my Thermos brand travel mug kept my Colombian dark roast toasty hot. That coffee was a godsend.

It was late, I'd been up for a long time, and I still had a ways to go. With winds aloft, I had at least another hour of flying before I reached my private airstrip in Eminence. This time Debbie would be waiting up for me.

On the ride home, I had plenty of time to think about what had transpired over the last few days and how I'd handled the situation. True, I had done some bad things, but nobody was perfect. Under the circumstances, my behavior could be excused. Right?

Perhaps, but that didn't stop the feeling of remorse that swept through me.

What kind of man had I become? Telling lies about another man's wife? Jeez, I should have never done that. Words hurt. I vowed never to do that again. I prayed for forgiveness and hoped that karma wouldn't come back and haunt me for saying those terrible things about Sally.

I looked at my watch. Twenty minutes to touchdown in Eminence. By now, "Big Sam" would have splashed down and sunk to the bottom, and he'd be rolling down the sloped sea floor from Jeffrey's Ledge to his final resting place in Wilkinson Basin. When he reached bottom, he'd be under nine hundred feet of ocean, his galvanized chains securing him to the seabed to feed the critters forever.

---

## 35

DEBBIE and I sat at our cozy table for two by the fireplace in the Lakeview House lounge. Soft rock music played in the background, and we ogled each other over joined hands like lovesick teenagers. I raised up my frosty beer mug, clinked it softly against her wineglass, and smiled harder than I had in a long time.

We had been sharing a room here since yesterday. We were checking out tomorrow, and I was sure I'd remember this stay for the rest of my life. Eating, drinking, and great sex. She slid one hand under the table and walked it up my thigh, then looked at me with a sly grin.

"Ya know, you really know how to spoil a girl."

I grinned, the ear-to-ear kind. I could tell she was tipsy because she never complimented me like that unless she'd had a few drinks. No matter how many times a woman tells her man he's a great lover, it never gets old. I stuck my chest out, the pride oozing from my face.

We did lots of texting too. Me on Sam's phone, and she on the two stooges' phones. We'd been going back and forth since I'd dropped Sam off, replicating the stupid shit these three Neanderthals sent to each other so that their associates would think they were still alive. We even had a contest going to see who could come up with the dumbest lines. We were about tied.

In between the texts to each other, I'd managed to send out a few to one of Sam's associates, Tough Tommy.

Sam: How you doing?

Tommy: Can't complain. Hows your trip

Sam: Barely surviving with these two numbskulls

Tommy: Better you then me

Sam: Might have that way out for us

Tommy: Way out? Whatcha talking about

Sam: You know, endgame that we spoke about

Tommy: What? Who is this?

Sam: Whatcha talking about who is this. I had that whatchamacallit that I told you about and it went well. I could get you out too if you still want

No response. I waited a few minutes, then texted Tommy again.

Sam: You okay?

Still no answer. Two minutes later, Fatty's phone vibrated. Debbie picked it up, read the text, and started to type. I slid my chair over to get closer to her and look over her shoulder to see her Shakespearean replies.

Tommy: You with Sam?

Bruno: Yeah, eating dinner. Good fuckin food here. What's up? You okay?

Tommy: Yeah, I'm fine. Sam's acting sorta funny

Bruno: Whatcha talking about?

Tommy: He's saying things that don't make any cents

Bruno: He's just trying to save your ass you numbskull

Tommy: What? Call me!

She powered off the phone. "Let him think about that for a while."

She topped off her sentence with her Hollywood smile. Skinny Jerry's phone vibrated. She looked down and read it. "Hmm, it's from a 'Tommy.'" She faked a surprised look on her face. "You want this?" She held the phone out to me.

"No, thanks, babe, you're doing a great job."

Tommy: Where you at?

Jerry: Dinner. You okay?

Tommy: Of course I'm okay. Wise everybody asking if I'm okay?

She placed the phone down on the table and took a sip of wine. She gestured towards the phone. "Let him think for a minute."

I nodded my appreciation. "Damn. You are good."

Tommy: You their?

Jerry: Sam didn't tell you?

Tommy: Tell me what?

Jerry: He can get us all out. Better call him

Two seconds after she hit send, Sam's phone rang. I let it go to voice mail. Tommy tried calling a few more times, and I shut the phone off for some peace and quiet.

We finished dinner and took our drinks back to our room. Debbie grabbed her iPod and turned on some Barry White. She showered while I double-checked that the three stooges' phones were off and stuffed them in my lead-shielded bag. I threw our phones in the bag too. I covered the flat-screen TV with a towel before getting naked and slipping into bed. Wouldn't want to give any of those HFS workers an inferiority complex.

Debbie came out of the bathroom. Naked.

# 36

THE TWO OF them looked like Hollywood's version of government stupids. Navy suits, dark red ties, sunglasses, white skin, midforties or maybe older. I made them as soon as they pulled up my driveway in their navy-blue Ford Taurus. Christ. What did these FBI hammerheads want?

I watched them through the feed of the security camera on my laptop. They exited the Ford, looked around, and made their way up my front steps.

I couldn't resist, and decided to play a little joke on them. I pulled out my Glock.

Before they had a chance to knock on my front door I swung it opened and pressed my Glock against the forehead of the first one.

"You're trespassing."

I swear I could see his pupils dilate through his Ray

Bans. I smelled shit too, but the odor faded fast so they must
have just farted. Guess my Dirty Harry imitation wasn't
good enough. I made a mental note to brush up on that
before I used it again.

They both raised their hands in surrender and the lead
guy let his ID fall open. "Whoa. Heh. Uhh... Leo Kennedy,
FBI. You can put the gun down. We're looking for Sheriff
Lamburt." His voice cracked like an excited teenager who
just found his father's stash of *Penthouse* magazines.

I studied his ID, my eyes going from it, to his face, half
a dozen times. I enjoyed seeing the sweat gather on his
upper lip. I nodded acceptance and smiled. "Sorry, fellas,
we've been having some Amish gang trouble here lately
and I wasn't expecting visitors. Can't be too careful, you
know."

They turned and looked at each other, seeming to
wonder if I was serious or not. I holstered my Glock and
stuck out my hand with my best used car salesman smile.
"Sheriff Lamburt, good to meet you fellas."

Their handshakes were limp and moist. Yuck. Sometimes I hated my job.

"Do you always answer your door pointing your gun at
people?" Kennedy asked. His tone was harsh, a real tough
talker now that he knew I wasn't going to blow his head off.

"No."

I stepped to the side of the doorway to let them pass.
"Come on in and warm up. It's cold out there."

They followed me inside. I gestured to the kitchen table.

"Sit. Make yourselves at home. Want anything to drink? Water, coffee, bourbon?"

"No, thanks. Can I use your bathroom?" the second agent asked.

"Sure, down the hall, first door on the left."

"Thanks." He walked away. I swear he was walking funny...

I made small talk with Kennedy while waiting for the other agent to clean his panties. He returned a few minutes later, looking more relaxed and at ease, and joined us at the table.

Kennedy turned to me. "We're trying to locate an undercover special agent who has gone missing."

My heart skipped a beat. Deep down, I'd feared that one of Ostrich Boy's entourage could be an undercover agent, but I didn't want to think about it. You always ran that risk, especially when HFS turned up a light criminal record for the guy. But there was no way for me to be sure. I mean, what was I supposed to do? Pull him aside and say, "Psst. Hey, buddy, wink wink. Do you work for the FBI?"

I did my best to sound surprised and appear interested. "Oh?"

"Yeah, he was last seen in Summit." He reached inside his suit breast pocket and took out a photo. He laid it down on the table. I looked into the eyes of the skinny guy who was lying under tons of dirt at the bottom of my well.

"This is Special Agent Jerry Skillman."

*Was.*

"Haven't seen him," I said.

"We know he was at the Red Barn, and we also know that you were present at the same time."

"Really? Huh. The Red Barn? When? And who told you?"

"We tracked his cell phone, and we think something may have happened to him while he was there with his associates. All three have gone missing. Earlier today, we interviewed the workers and some of the patrons of the Red Barn. They were surprisingly standoffish towards us. One little old lady even told us to go fuck ourselves. After she grabbed my ass."

"Oh my." I held my hand to my mouth and feigned concern over Frances's use of such terrible language, then I hit them with the fake news story I'd created on the Internet over the last few days. "Wait. Does this have anything to do with those three mobsters that bugged out and joined the witness protection plan?"

"What? Where'd you hear about that?"

"It's all over the Internet." Which was true. A few well-placed tweets and Facebook posts on some popular accounts that I hacked into was all it had taken to create the fake news story of the year. Even the President tweeted about the missing trio...

People were so gullible. They just retweeted and reposted stuff that they had no idea was false, spreading the virus of misinformation until it blossomed into reality.

I'm sure Sam's mob associates were shocked to hear the

news, but since it was all over the place *and* some of his associates really did rat him out just a few weeks ago, it was believable.

The FBI couldn't comment on who decided to join the squealing rat club, which meant that Sam's buddies would be even more convinced that my fake news stories were real.

HFS also turned up a few interesting tidbits regarding the disappearance of one of Sam's crew, a fellow called Tough Tommy. I'm guessing that someone in Sam's crew was "tipped off," ahem, about the plans Sam and Tommy were hatching. Once the seed was planted in the paranoid brains of his fellow mobsters, it was an easy call to take a look at Tommy's cell phone.

The texts with the missing trio were read, analyzed, debated, and a conclusion was drawn. It was all over for Tough Tommy. Too bad he'd never learned how to erase a text chain...

Kennedy stared at me, his forehead furrowed in confusion. "We heard that rumor too. But I can assure you that since the FBI runs the witness protection program, we know who joins it."

I stared blankly at him.

He looked away and continued, "Do you remember anything unusual that happened at the Red Barn last weekend?"

"No, not at all. Sorry I can't be more helpful."

I stood up and showed them the door. They each

reached into their leather card-carrying cases and handed me one of their business cards.

"Please call if you hear anything."

"Yes, I most certainly will." *Don't hold your breath.*

I closed the door behind them and threw their cards in the fireplace.

## 37

My cell phone rang. It was Mary Sue's mom, Meredith.

"Hi, Mer."

"Can we talk?"

"Sure. What's going on?"

"Not on the phone, in person. Tiby's Coffee Shop? About four?"

"Sure. See you then."

*What was that about?*

I knew the second I walked in and saw her face that something was wrong. She smiled, and that was always a great sight, but I could tell by the way her face was contorted that something wasn't right. She got out of her chair and hugged me. Tight. That was new. We'd gotten together many times over the years, but she'd never been this touchy-feely with me. She looked up at me, tears welling in her red-rimmed eyes.

"You look great, Jack."

I pulled out a chair and sat down. "Thanks, you too. Been too long. Um, hey, you okay?"

"Yeah, I'm just glad to see you," she sniffled and finger-wiped a tear from her cheek. "I know what happened."

"Excuse me?"

"I know what you did, and I wanted to thank you for saving our daughter. In person."

My heart skipped two beats. I was speechless, so she continued; "We have security cameras in our house."

*Oh. Shit.*

"Really?" I replied.

She rolled her eyes. "Yes. Really. When Stu and I returned from Key West I went to do my usual house cleaning, and I noticed that my cleaning supplies were almost empty. They were full when we left. So I figured I'd better, what's that term the sportscaster's always use, 'go to the video tape?' So I saw everything that happened in our kitchen..."

"Oh."

"I wanted to thank you."

"Okay."

"But that's not all." She looked down at the floor. "This is really hard for me, but after seeing the video, I needed to finally tell you, so here goes." She took a deep breath and looked me in the eye. "I never regretted our affair. Not for a second. Mary Sue's just so special. She's so much like you, and I can't tell you how happy I am to have her in my life. And... I've loved you since high school."

My jaw dropped and bounced off the table three times before I regained control. "What?"

"It's true. I made a mistake marrying Stu. He's great and all. A fantastic provider, a great husband, a great dad too. But he doesn't make my heart skip a beat when he walks into the room. Like you do. Did. I mean."

After a long pause to think about the bomb she'd just dropped on me, I continued the conversation. "So why didn't you marry me instead? You knew how I felt about you."

"I panicked. I'm sorry, but you were such a rich and spoiled carefree party animal, I never thought you would amount to anything. With the baby coming, I needed someone I could count on. Someone reliable. Plus I figured you were just doing the manly thing—you know, offering to marry the woman who you got pregnant. And of course the great sex only clouded your feelings for me. And I had this commitment to Stu. I couldn't just back out of our wedding." She looked at me and shrugged.

Maybe it was because I would have never found Cheryl if Meredith and I had gotten hitched. Or maybe I'd never really loved Meredith as much as I'd thought I did, but I didn't see any reason to keep beating ourselves up over this. No more living in the past.

I let out a sigh. "You're right. I can't say I blamed you. In fact, I'd say you made the right decision. Stuart's a good man." I quickly changed the subject. "How's Mary Sue?"

She hesitated for a second, then took a deep breath as if in resignation that it was time to move on. "Oh, she's fine. I hope you're not upset, but I wanted her to be able to vent, so I told her I saw the security video. She cried on my shoulder for a while, but after that she's been fine."

"Good. I'm glad that you told her. It's important that she be able to confide in you. She's a great kid. You and Stuart deserve a lot of credit. You two did a great job raising her."

"Thanks, but she's got your spunk, your fire, your character, I see it in her eyes every day, and I tear up just thinking about it." She dabbed at her eyes with a napkin.

I looked at her, unsure of what to say. I'd been friends with her in high school and had always liked her. A lot. But I'd been too shy to act on it.

I'd found she had feelings for me when we'd gotten drunk at a holiday party one year when I came home from Notre Dame for Christmas break. We'd wound up having sex in the backseat of my BMW—no easy feat for someone as big as me, mind you. And, she'd gotten pregnant.

To make matters worse, she was engaged to be married to Stuart. We were horrified. Her at being pregnant, me at that, plus the fact that I'd gotten drunk and slept with another man's woman.

I would have regretted it, except that Mary Sue came with the deal, and she was something to thank God for. And I did. Every night I dropped to my knees and prayed hard for her. To guide and watch over her. To keep her healthy and to help her make good strong decisions in life. To keep her "parents" healthy and wise. I've never been a very religious man, but so far so good.

"Do you think Stuart's ever suspected that Mary Sue wasn't his daughter?"

"No. At least I don't think so. I never told him, of course, but he is a smart guy. If he does know, he never let on. And he does kind of look like you." She winked at me and took a sip of her coffee.

"He really is a good man."

"Yes, he is." She napkined another tear away.

"Why this? And why now?"

"Because I watched the whole video. I saw what happened, Jack. I don't know how it started, I'm guessing it's a Red Barn thing, but that doesn't matter. What matters is that you stopped it." She flashed me a small, comfortable smile, and held my eyes. "And I read the papers. I read about the three missing mobsters. I recognized the one from the video. He's a bad man."

She looked around and leaned in close, like she was preparing to pass me Russian nuclear weapon secrets. "Sammy. Sammy something," she whispered. "The papers say they went off grid and did that witness protection thingy. But we know better." She smiled and winked at me.

She reached across the table and grabbed my hands and squeezed them tight.

"Thank you for saving her. I know how it works with

those mob people. How it'd never end if you followed the rule of the law. Something that you pride yourself in doing."

*If she only knew...*

"Did Stuart see the security video?"

"No. Soon as I watched it, I deleted it. Nobody will ever know, as long as that wussy ex-boyfriend keeps his mouth shut. Aren't you worried about him telling?" She laughed and shook her head. She paused for a second, and a seriousness returned to her face that I rarely saw in her. She leaned in close again. More top-secret highly classified document passing. She whispered, "At one point, I thought you were going to shoot him."

I laughed it off. "Ha. I guess you haven't heard? I convinced Harold to join the Marines. He reports to Paris Island in a few weeks. We're going to have a going away party for him next Saturday at the Red Barn. I hope that you and Stuart can make it."

"Oh, that's good. Yeah, Stu is off next Saturday. And he always liked Harold, so I'm sure that he'd like to go."

"Excellent," I stood up to leave and gave her a hug and a smile. "Just keep him away from Frances."

# EPILOGUE

WHILE I WAS busy dumping Fat Sam into the Atlantic, Debbie found London still alive so she rushed him to the Vet for an emergency operation.

He'd taken a bullet to his chest and wound up expiring on the operating table, but the Doc told me that his heart condition was a lot worse than he thought, and even though the bullet did kill him, his time was very limited. As in 'I'm surprised he lasted this long' limited. That would explain how tired he seemed all of the time.

I couldn't help but admire him even more now, going out in a blaze of glory like that. Leave it to London to come through one final time and save the day. I could only hope that I would be that lucky when my time was up.

I built a coffin for him out of some pressure treated lumber. I put his bed in the coffin and laid him down on his right side, his favorite way to sleep. He looked so peaceful.

Debbie tossed in a few of his treats, along with his chew toys, and I placed a photo of Cheryl next to him to keep him company.

We buried him right next to my hammock, so that he'd always be by my side.

A week from Tuesday I have an appointment to get my first tattoo. It's going on my chest. When I showed Jamie at the tattoo shop in Cobleskill the photo of a head shot of London that Cheryl took when he was only a year old, she smiled and nodded. "Nice."


THE END


TURN the page to get a FREE preview of Airliner Down!

**FREE PREVIEW; AIRLINER DOWN**
**CHAPTER 1**

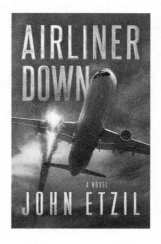

December 27, 9:43 p.m.

   Two hours before the event

As the big airliner climbed past twenty-four thousand feet,
the air pressure detonator worked exactly as planned. In

retrospect, it was all too easy. A small metal box, about the size of a child's shoebox, held the components of the bomb: a nine-volt battery, a small brick of C-4 plastic explosive, a sealed glass capsule, and a digital timer.

The box was attached to the forward bulkhead in the unpressurized nose cone of the airliner. The reduction in air pressure as the airliner climbed in altitude caused the air inside the thimble-sized glass capsule to expand until it burst. The shattering of the capsule completed an electrical circuit and started the digital timer.

In two hours, the timer would reach zero, and the nine-volt battery would fire an electrical charge to the blasting cap in the C-4. The blasting cap would detonate the C-4, and the explosion would rip apart the big airliner, sending the three hundred plus holiday vacationers to their deaths.

# AIRLINER DOWN CHAPTER 2

Five hours before the event

Inside Terminal Six at Los Angeles International Airport, off-duty airline pilot Kevin McSorley rolled his carry-on luggage over the gray tiled floor towards the check-in station at his departure gate. Midevening on a Tuesday in the week between Christmas and New Year's was a quiet time for the airlines, and he had the terminal mostly to himself. Off-key, he sang out loud, "Deck the halls with boughs of holly," as he made his way through the terminal. He daydreamed about his upcoming flight to Hawaii and the six nights he would spend in a five-star hotel with a beautiful woman. His woman. "Tis the season to be jolly..."

His iPhone vibrated in his pocket, indicating a new text message. He retrieved it, and as if on cue to verify their strong mental connection, it was Margie.

Margie: Just got in, hotel rocks!

Kevin: cool, you naked yet?

Margie: Still in the lobby

Kevin: is that a yes or no?

Margie: Sophomoric

Kevin: just at gate now

Margie: Wow, u r early. Can't wait, eh?

Kevin: u bet, baby!

Margie: Hitting the gym and then the lounge for food

Kevin: don't pick up any strangers

Margie: Define stranger??

Kevin: sophomoric

Margie: Kisses. Hurry here!

Kevin: XOXO all over

Margie: Waiting up for u w cold beer

Kevin: nice! send photo

Margie: Of coors light?

Kevin: of u naked

Margie: No, use your imagination

Kevin: roger. gotta check in now, babe. Kisses

Margie: Luv u

Kevin: u 2 ;-)

Kevin smiled, pocketed his phone, and headed over towards the gate that had "Flight 2262 LAX–HNL: On Time" illuminated above the check-in counter. He looked around at the near-empty terminal and checked the time: 6:47 p.m. He had arrived early for his 9:15 p.m. flight and looked forward to putting on his headphones and relaxing to some classical music for the first time in a while.

Kevin recognized the slim brunette ticket agent at his gate as soon as he spotted her. Tess. Her dark skin and long, slightly wavy black hair that reached down to the middle of her back were a perfect complement to her bright smile and pretty features. Close to thirty, she still showed off the athletic remnants of being a collegiate swimmer in the form of a tight body, something every man within fifty feet took notice of.

"Hi, Tess," he said.

Tess stopped what she was doing, looked up at him, and greeted him with a smile. "Well, hello, Captain." She looked him up and down, and a look of snarkiness overtook her as she noticed his unusual attire: sneakers, jeans, and a button-down Hawaiian-style shirt along with an LA Dodgers baseball cap. "Wow, someone's letting their hair down," she said in reference to his normally streamlined and stoic captainly appearance. "Will you be joining us to Hawaii tonight?" she asked.

"Yes, I will." Kevin smiled back at her, leaned on the counter, and handed her his buddy pass, the airline employee equivalent of a general admission ticket. Even if his flight was sold out, the buddy pass allowed him to sit on the fold-down jump seat in the cockpit. The jump seat was small, and the two-person cockpit was overly snug when a third person rode along, but it got the job done.

"Damn," Tess said. An exaggerated pout appeared on her otherwise perfect face. "Wish I was going to Hawaii. I did my friend a favor and traded flights with her." Her almond-shaped green eyes looked right at him. "Now I'm sorry I did that. Your flight crew has a three-day layover in Hawaii, and a three-day layover with you would have been fun."

*Gulp.* Kevin's heart skipped a beat. When she turned on the charm, she had the ability to make him feel like a nervous freshman, and despite his allegiance to Margie, his brain shut down and Margie was but a faint thought. Excitement churned in his stomach like a runaway freight train, and his mind was consumed for the moment by Tess.

"Yeah, that would have been fun." Kevin felt guilty about his enticement and tried to be nonchalant. "But don't worry, I have a feeling I'll be passing through these parts again soon."

"How long are you staying in Hawaii?"

"Seven days."

"Wow, nice." She smiled at him and leaned over the counter to get closer to him, her face just inches from his. "Hey, I'm on break in about twenty. Can I buy you a Coke before you leave on your little holiday vacay? Your flight's not leaving for a while."

"Uhm, not tonight. I, uh, have some work to do before we board," he lied, and stepped back slightly to create some distance between them. He was on the verge of caving in and needed some space. "But I'll take a rain check." He followed up his rejection with a thousand-watt smile.

She leaned in closer. Some of her hair brushed against his face and feathered his nose as he inhaled. He closed his eyes and savored the moment. He thought of Margie. Guilt came, he inhaled, and the guilt disappeared. God, she smelled so good.

"You know," she whispered in his ear, her breath warm and perfect, "we can go to the pilots' lounge. I'll show you my tattoos."

Tattoos were a common thread between them, and they discussed them often. "All of them?" he replied, his nonexistent impulse control once again rearing its ugly head and sabotaging his potential relationship with a member of the opposite sex. What was he doing?

"Every. Single. One." She punctuated each word, and Kevin felt his composure wavering.

Thinking of Margie, he sputtered, "Oh, man. I'd love to, but it's just not a good time. Sorry." And with a meek shoulder shrug, he waited and looked at her with a sheepish smile.

With a deep sigh, she looked down at the papers in front of her and finished her work. It was clear to Kevin that she wasn't used to being rejected by the opposite sex and that she didn't take it well. After a few seconds, she regained her happy demeanor and smiled at him as she handed him back his buddy pass with his seat assignment. "Have a great flight, sir."

"Thanks." He took his buddy pass, grabbed his bag, and rolled it away. He fought the urge to look at his seat assignment to see if she'd stuck him in the ass of the airliner, next to the bathroom.

After finding a seat far enough away from Tess so that he could focus on his work, he broke out his laptop. Since FAA regs mandated that airline pilots could only fly one hundred hours per month, they didn't really work that much. Most wound up flying eighty-five to ninety hours per month. That left them with plenty of free time for a pilot's two favorite pastimes—getting drunk, and chasing women. Plural.

Kevin had decided early in his career that it was in his best long-term financial interest to have just one wife rather than supporting a handful of women who would eventually collect alimony from him. So to keep himself busy, and out of trouble, he'd opened an Internet store that sold pilots' supplies: sunglasses, watches, and other miscellaneous items that pilots found appealing. That had worked out well up until a few months ago—the one wife part, anyway.

He attempted to check his sales numbers for the day, but he couldn't focus on the spreadsheet. He was distracted by the encounter with Tess, and his mind drifted to his younger days. Days of opportunity.

But not now. There was too much going on in his life, and the last thing he needed was another emotional attachment. And make no mistake about it, intimacy with Tess would create an attachment that would make his personal situation look like World War III as opposed to a minor skirmish in the field.

Just the same, if she kept it up, he didn't know how much longer he'd be able to resist her.

# AIRLINER DOWN CHAPTER 3

Two hours and forty-five minutes before the event

Kevin was so excited about his trip to Hawaii that he forgot to check and see who his pilots were. He usually reviewed the flight crew lineup a few days ahead of time, and if he liked the guys, he'd sit up front in the cockpit and ride jump seat with them instead of sitting with the flying public in coach. Although uncomfortable, the little fold-down seat behind the captain's seat was tolerable for a thin person like Kevin.

He boarded the plane and looked into the cockpit, where he saw the first officer, Tom Burns, sitting in the right seat. He was chatting with a fellow in a dark suit that was standing behind the captain's seat. He didn't recognize the visitor, but Kevin had flown with Tom many times and thought of him as a good pilot. Equally important, Tom was a good cockpit mate. Sometimes the younger guys that had just gotten promoted to the bigger airliners were a little nervous or hesitant in their actions or decision making, oftentimes deferring to the more experienced captain. Kevin tolerated that, figuring that it was all part of their learning and getting comfortable with the big aircraft, but he could never tolerate a bad cockpit mate. He had compiled a mental list, a personal "No Fly With Me" list, of guys who never shut up, ranted about politics or bad exes, or were all-around miserable beings who made five hours next to them in the cockpit intolerable. Tom wasn't on that list.

The left seat, where the captain sat, was occupied by Captain Roy Peterson, a thirty-five-year veteran of the airlines. Roy turned in his seat and, with the agility of a man half his age, extricated himself from his chair. "Excuse me, gentlemen," he said as he made his way out of the cockpit.

"Bathroom already? No more coffee for you, old man," said Tom.

"You got that right," Roy said. "The caffeine might interfere with my midflight nap. Can't let that happen."

Tom sighed, closed his eyes, and smacked his forehead in pretend anguish at his peer's old joke. "Need new material, Captain."

Roy stepped out of the cockpit, his always present smile lighting up his face, and recognized Kevin right away. "Hey, young man," he said. "Nice to see you." He held out his hand and Kevin took it—his shake was strong and firm, like a man twenty years younger than his real age.

"Hi, Captain," Kevin said. "We going to have a smooth flight tonight? I need to catch up on some sleep."

"What, you're flying and you haven't checked the en route weather forecast?" the captain ribbed. "Seems like they'll hire anybody to drive these aluminum tubes these days."

"Ha, no, I've been a little preoccupied," said Kevin. *Yeah, with Margie.*

Roy paused, and a seriousness crept into his look, "Can I talk with you a second?" He waved Kevin away from the other passengers and over to a quiet spot in the galley.

"Sure."

"This might not be any of my business, but I heard about you and Patty, and I just wanted to tell you that I'm sorry."

"Thanks, I appreciate that."

"Don't feel bad if you need to take some time off. Clear your head and all."

"Yeah, I was thinking about that...but you know how it is. Work is good for the soul. Keeps your mind off your troubles."

"True, just as long as your troubles don't interfere with your work. But I trust that you'll know if that happens. If you ever need anything, just let me know."

"Thanks, I will."

"So how long are you staying in Hawaii?" The smile came back and Roy put his hand on Kevin's shoulder.

"Seven days."

"Nice. Bringing in the New Year in Hawaii is a real treat. Elizabeth and I did that a few years ago. It was a great time. The Hawaiian people are just so friendly."

"Yeah, I'm really looking forward to it."

"Most of our crew will be laying over for three days at the Hilton. If you want to hang with us, we have some sight-seeing planned for later in the day tomorrow, followed up with dinner and drinks at this awesome restaurant that I discovered a few months ago. You're welcome to join us."

"Thanks, Cap. I'm good, though. Just going to relax and hang poolside for a few days."

"Roger that. If you change your mind, the offer is always open."

"Okay, thanks again." Kevin shook his hand and made his way back to the seat that Tess had assigned him. At the ass end of the aircraft.

Right next to the bathroom.

He appreciated Roy's gesture and he was going to miss him when he left. He hoped he'd get one more flight tour with Roy before he retired, but he kept getting shut out on his bids. The monthly bid schedule for pilot routes favored the guys with the most seniority, and most of the pilots with higher seniority than Kevin also wanted to fly with Roy one more time before he retired. Kevin had no way of knowing it, but he would never fly with Roy again.

He sat down in his aisle seat, loosely fastened his seat belt, and thought of Margie. Seven days of uninterrupted quality time spent with his soul mate. Margie's uplifting energy was the perfect remedy to his marital woes.

His daydreaming was interrupted by his vibrating phone. He took it out and saw a text message from Margie.

Margie: Room is awesome

Kevin: not flying to HNL for the room

Margie: Me neither. Taking a bath.

Kevin: alone?

Margie: Ass

Kevin: hot crew on board this flight

Margie: Bring 1 with u

Kevin: ur a perfect girlfriend!

Margie: Make sure he's young AND fit

Kevin: uhm...meant SHE crew!!!

Margie: Oh! How silly of me. Just kidding...tee hee

Kevin: now Im bringing 2

Margie: Ha! Better take your Viagra!

Kevin: we'll c

Margie: Might have 2 nap, wake me when u come

Kevin: I will w/ XOXO all over

Margie: Sleep on the flight, NO flirting! Bring energy. NO excuses!

Kevin: kisses baby

Margie: XOXO!!

Kevin heard the solid thunk of the cabin door as it was closed and secured in place. A few minutes later, he felt the firm nudge as the tug connected with the nose gear of the big airliner and pushed it back from its gate. He heard the familiar soothing sound of the jet engines starting, and the aircraft started its taxi.

One of the ladies from the cabin crew came on the intercom and began her preflight announcements to the passengers, which included the locations of the emergency exits, the reminder that your seat cushion was a flotation device, and best of all, instructions on how a seat belt worked, just in case there was a Neanderthal on board.

Captain Roy came on the mike and, with the authority that only a seasoned airline pilot possessed, advised the flight crew to take their seats: "We're number one for takeoff."

On the runway, the two engines spooled up smoothly and the familiar feeling of being pushed back in his seat as the airliner accelerated made Kevin feel at home. The tires bumped along the runway expansion strips, getting softer and softer as the wings started to rise and take on the weight of the big airliner, and then silence as the nose rose and the massive two hundred and fifty tons of machine defied the laws of physics and took flight. The landing gear was raised, completing its journey into the wheel wells with a solid thunk, and the flaps were retracted.

The symphony of events that culminated in flight helped Kevin shake off the negativity of the past, and he plugged his headset into his iPhone and relaxed to some classical music. He closed his eyes and thought of Margie, and his mood elevated even higher. He relished the feel of her breath on his cheek, the excited way she hugged him when she saw him, the tenderness in her touch. She was perfect for him in every way.

Except that she was married.

# FREE BOOK EXCLUSIVE TO MY READERS

Join my VIP Readers Group and get Fast Justice!

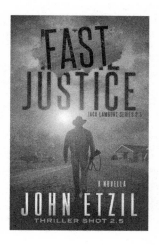

FREE - Jack Lamburt 2.5 Fast Justice

JohnEtzil.com

## ACKNOWLEDGMENTS

To my readers: **THANK YOU!**

One of the rewards of being a writer is hearing from fans. If you have a free minute, I'd appreciate a review.

Look for another Jack Lamburt adventure in the fall of 2017. Until then... ;-)

# ABOUT THE AUTHOR

John was introduced to Agatha Christie in the late seventies, and became a life long reader of mystery and thrillers after he read Murder On The Orient Express.

His favorite book is Deliverance. His favorite authors include Nelson DeMille, Russell Blake, fellow New Jerseyan AND Hungarian Janet Evanovich, Barry Eisler, Max Allan Collins, J.A. Konrath, Wayne Stinnett, Mark Dawson, Lawrence Block, and Lee Goldberg, but he'll entertain anything with airplanes, Jiu Jitsu, badass women with tattoos, big manly dogs, and tons of action!

His first novel, Airliner Down, was drafted in the summer of 2015. After numerous rewrites, he released it in March of 2017.

Fatal Justice; Vigilante Justice Thriller Series 2 with Jack Lamburt, was written during the Airliner Down rewrites and also released in March of 2017.

FAST Justice; Vigilante Justice Thriller Series 2.5 with Jack Lamburt, is a FREE 20K word "Thriller Shot"

Urban Justice; Vigilante Justice Thriller Series 3 with Jack Lamburt, was released in November of 2017.

URGENT Justice; Vigilante Justice Thriller Series 3.5 with Jack Lamburt, is a 28K word "Thriller Shot" and was released in October of 2018.

First Justice; Vigilante Justice Thriller Series 1 with Jack Lamburt, was released in December of 2019.

John is a commercial rated pilot with over twenty years of flight experience. He is an avid weight trainer and holds a purple belt in Gracie Jiu Jitsu.

He currently resides in New Jersey with his bad ass wife, two teenage sons, and two medium sized dogs.

www.JohnEtzil.com

Made in the USA
Las Vegas, NV
16 June 2021

24868394R00125